Willesden Herald
New Short Stories 11

www.newshortstories.com

Published simultaneously in the United States
and the United Kingdom in 2019
by Pretend Genius Press

Editor: Stephen Moran
Cover photo and design: Stratos Fountoulis

ISBN 978-0-9995277-6-4

Willesden Herald

New Short Stories 11

Editor: Stephen Moran

www.NewShortStories.com

Contents

Introduction

Frequently depicted as the novel's poor cousin, the short story is often under-read and definitely under-estimated. For many, it is seen as a stepping stone towards writing that weightier piece of work, the novel, as if size, or word count, are the means of defining a worthwhile piece of literature. Yet in truth, for its longevity alone the short story deserves greater recognition than this, it deserves a higher status in the literary cannon. From earliest times, the short story has been part of our lives and still remains firmly rooted in our many cultures. These narratives may be shorter, they may not take up as much space as a novel, yet even so they help us mark our place in the world and by doing this they connect us.

The short story is, as V. S. Pritchett explains, 'exquisitely difficult,' to write. With such a legacy, no wonder it is tricky. It is entitled to be. For undoubtedly the short story is a hard taskmaster. It asks a lot from the writer. And whilst content, style and genre are open to any and all, there is no room for lingering wordiness. It wants us to be swift in our telling. The short story favours the writers of crisp, fresh prose. Every paragraph, every sentence and every word must have a job to do and be doing it. Yet no matter the length, and that can be variable, there must be a story arc: conflict, crisis and resolution. These three words represent the bones of every story. They support it. Forget them at your peril, for they bring about change and there must be change. Change is crucial. Without it there is no story. Without change there is only an anecdote.

Then again, the short story is the form best suited to the misfits, to those who struggle, both emotionally and physically, and to those who find they are alone. This is where the beauty of the short story lies. It relishes characters who are out of step, the ones who can be seen, slightly lost, stumbling around in the margins. The short story suits a character on the back foot. Also, amongst the discomfort and unease, perhaps this is where we make the strongest connections, at a time when we are anxious for characters shadowed by impending danger. Perhaps, this is when we realise the short story gives a voice to those midnight thoughts that plague us all, and we recognise them.

Most of all, the short story embodies intensity. Those moments of sharp detail which bring a story to life. Often it is a series of resonating images, finely drawn and deeply embedded, like a thread weaving through the narrative. Or intensity may be found in a deftly written undercurrent running below the surface of a story like a series of whispers never quite heard. Because the short story is playful in its intensity, it makes us work for our understanding. It shows only what is needed, and leaves so much unsaid. It is here we uncover the 'not-telling,' where the words are carefully chosen and adroitly placed, like sleight of hand, to reveal another story. This is the magic: in discovering the secret story and exposing the one which is never meant to be told. And for me, this is where the heart of the story lies. It is to be found tucked down, beating deep within the intensity.

Because it packs so much into such a small space,

the short story can be a slippery creature. It requires the close attention of the reader. It is unforgiving to the writer. It demands a fresh eye and an understanding of nuance. Get this wrong and it languishes like a damp squib, disappointing and soon forgotten. Above all, in order for the reader to believe, the short story demands to be written with truth. And when it is, then it is certainly no poor cousin languishing in the shadows of that thicker book, the novel. Nor is it a new kid on the block. Rather it is a force to be reckoned with. The short story may be small but it is a fierce piece of storytelling and we should never undervalue it.

Happily, for both readers and writers, the short story is very much alive and kicking and would appear to being going through a resurgence of popularity. Much has been said about why. Perhaps, it is the brevity that fits into our busy lifestyles: a short story can be read on the train or bus, in a lunchtime. And as there is no need for a long commitment, it fills a desire for immediate gratification. Alongside this is our growing need, driven by social media, for instant connections, those momentary touches on the lives of others. This too the short story satisfies. Or perhaps the form is best suited to times of unease, its intensity reflecting the tensions in our world, its displaced characters resonating with our own feelings of apprehension. Perhaps it is most popular when it echoes our fears.

With all this in mind, it has been a pleasure to read the fifteen stories gathered together for New Short Stories 11. In their own way, each has contributed to the creation of an anthology rich with a diversity of tone and voice. The stories are drawn together from different corners of the world, their narratives firmly rooted in place by distinctive dialogue and fine, subtle detail. They give glimpses into unfamiliar worlds and unknown lives. The characters struggle, they creep around in the margins, and yes, there is change. Each piece has its own style, has shown skilful storytelling and each has earned their part in the book. Thank you to all the writers, I have enjoyed the connections.

Gina Challen
November 2019

Miss Maughan

JL Bogenschneider

On Tuesday, Miss Maughan left us three times. The first time, she ran out of the classroom mid-way through English. We joked that she was hungover, or worse – this from Joseph Arbour – that she had the runs. The whole class laughed before collapsing into unrestrained chatter, but we quietened down when she returned.

The second time, she almost knocked over the vase of wildflowers on her desk that she replenished at the beginning of each week. The jokes were fewer but our excitement at being abandoned again led to an outbreak of minor pandemonium. After the third time, when we were left unsupervised for the longest, we sat in silence. When our headteacher, Mr Dalton, entered the class-room around twenty minutes later, he seemed almost suspicious of our subdued state and stared around for some moments before addressing us, as though he were expecting some kind of trap.

"Miss Maughan," he began, "will not be present for the rest of the day." He allowed his words to sink in, accusingly. "Therefore I will be your teacher for the afternoon," – there was an audible groan from the back row – "and as I have enough work of my own to do, you will study in silence."

Miss Maughan could be strict when she needed to be but she didn't mind so much if you spoke with your neighbour during the lesson. I wondered how I was going to be able to tell Martin Olsen, who sat behind me, about the ant nest I'd found in the gym cupboard. I could have written a note, but Mr Dalton had an eerie awareness of movement, as if – even though he was concentrating on a report on the desk – some invisible antenna was beaming out and receiving signals from all around him. I thought of the RKO radio tower when I thought of him; imposing, old and grey. There was a general shuffling of papers from everyone and then, at a glance from Mr Dalton, we bowed our heads to our books.

†

Later on, back home, my mother was in the kitchen, chopping vegetables and humming a wandering, endless tune.

"Miss Maughan went home sick today," I told her. "We had Mr Dalton instead."

The subtle change of afternoon into evening was marked by the exit of my mother to work. I slumped in an armchair in front of the television. We'd been given homework by Mr Dalton but I didn't even think of doing it because Miss Maughan wouldn't know it'd been assigned. When my father came home, I moved from the chair to the floor. We said nothing to each other. He didn't like to do much of anything after work but sit until he fell asleep and had to be woken up to go to bed. At around nine my mother would come in and shoo me upstairs so she could have her own time of peace.

†

In the morning, Miss Maughan wasn't there. After the bell, we filed in, falling silent one-by-one as we saw her vacant desk. Taking our seats, we fell to speculating if she was still sick and then, this from Joseph Arbour again, "Maybe she died."

There was a nervous laughter around the room as we considered this, a humour we didn't want to comprehend and then someone – I didn't see who – piped up from the front.

"Did anyone do Mr Dalton's homework?"

The air froze and a murmur made its way around the room as everyone admitted to everyone else that, no – in fact – they hadn't, and we awaited the oncoming storm.

When the door opened, our collective breath held, the dread figure of Mr Dalton failed to appear. Instead, a small, round woman entered, bundled in an oversized cardigan with a shawl draped around her neck. She made for the desk and sat down, reaching for the box of tissues that was kept – always untouched – in front of Miss Maughan. She grabbed a handful and blew her nose. When she withdrew her hand we saw that her face was a distinct hue of cracked red; the sort of colour that indicated a lifetime of minor ill-health. After disposing of the tissues in the bin beneath the desk she spent some moments rearranging the items upon it, pushing papers to one side and moving the vase with the wildflowers to the far edge, near the window, where it threatened to fall if pushed a little further, like bunched up coins in a penny arcade. She looked up and seemed surprised to see us, as though we were the ones out of place and not her. She cleared her throat, making a gurgling noise, and spoke with a voice like cold glass.

"Good morning. My name is Mrs Tipps. I will be your substitute until further notice. I have been provided with a lesson plan but have also been given permission to direct proceedings as I see fit. Therefore we will commence this morning's session with a discussion on Current Events."

Immediately, I disliked her. She used unnecessary words when simpler ones would do and you could tell that when she said things like Current Events, she meant them to be capitalised. I also didn't care for her saying she'd be our substitute *until further notice*. I didn't know what that meant and thought about raising my hand to ask, but she'd already asked Wendy Bayham to talk about a Current Event.

I thought back to the previous evening. There'd been a news item about someone who'd killed their baby just after it was born. They were trying to decide whether or not they should be sent to prison, or if they'd killed their baby because of some reason I couldn't understand. There was also sports news, but I didn't think that would be considered a Current Event, although it met the technical criteria.

Wendy had spoken about something was going on in her church that weekend, which was stupid because Current Events happened in the news on the television or in the papers; they weren't things that happened to us. But Mrs Tipps had already moved onto the next person. I counted heads to see when it would be my turn and hoped no-one else would mention the baby thing. I was thinking about this so much that I failed to hear what anyone else was saying and, when called upon, simply had to hope it hadn't been brought up. When I'd finished, Mrs Tipps stared at me, her head cocked to one side. She took a handful of tissues, told us to discuss our Current Events with the person next to us, then left the room.

We were becoming accustomed to being abandoned in this way. Joseph Arbour came straight out with it.

"I think she killed her own baby. It's the only reason she'd walk out like that."

"No," someone else said, "She's got what Miss Maughan's got. She'll be gone by the end of the morning."

Meanwhile, Martin tapped me on the back. He

leaned over his desk.

"She's called Mrs Tipps."

"So?" I said.

"*Mrs* Tipps" he repeated. "Someone *married* her!"

I laughed. I liked Martin because he noticed things no-one else did and I began to tell him about the ant nest but at that moment Mrs Tipps returned and the lesson resumed.

The rest of the morning passed without incident. While everybody else spoke, I wondered if male teachers had different titles if they weren't married and if the other male teachers – there were only two at our school – were called Mr because they *were* married. This led me to think that Miss Maughan wasn't married, which I didn't see should be the case because she was nice. After everyone had contributed a Current Event, we reverted to the lesson plan and worked until break.

†

Outside in the yard we carried on as normal. I told Martin about the ant nest in the gym and we made plans to go there at the end of the day. The gym teacher, Mr Arthurs, would often allow us to stay until he closed up and didn't mind leaving us unsupervised. He was the sort of gym teacher who was overweight and smoked whilst sitting on the benches, sweating without exertion as he instructed us. I don't think I ever saw him use any of the equipment in the cupboard in my whole time at the school.

But, this plan agreed, we returned to the classroom. In our absence, Mrs Tipps had abandoned the set lesson in favour of a something she called a Social Experiment. She had us divide and line up into two groups; boys on one side of the room and girls on the other. Then she announced that, in the order in which we found ourselves, we were to select a partner from the other side.

"Life" she declared, "is all about finding a partner for oneself. It does one no harm to get a little practice in, in those nascent years before adolescence befalls us. Now, you–," she pointed to Joseph Arbour. "Choose."

Joseph look at her dumbly, "You mean I have to choose a girl?"

She looked at him like you would a dog that'd just messed the carpet.

"Yes, you must choose a girl. Unless," she posited slyly, "you would prefer to choose a boy?"

The class erupted into laughter at this, another humour we only part-grasped. Joseph reddened, but recovered enough to ask how he was to decide and Mrs Tipps answered airily, "Oh, just pick the one you like the best."

Joseph's coloured redoubled and I knew why, because earlier in the year he'd told me he liked Wendy Bayham; this, at that sexless age when boys liking girls was a cause for shame, but preferring boys – as evinced by the reaction to Mrs Tipp's earlier comment – was not something that could be admitted to either.

I looked at Joseph cautiously, wondering if he would pick Wendy or not. It was cruel, I thought, even then. I didn't see how he could answer: if he chose Wendy then it would be clear to everyone that he liked her, but if he didn't then he would feel that he'd somehow missed out on a chance to declare his childish love. I knew this was the case because it was how I felt about Wendy also.

Joseph's voice finally called out Wendy's name in a sullen tone. The room exploded with whistles and cat-calls, which Mrs Tipps quelled with her imperious voice before instructing the new couple to sit together in the front row.

Next it was James Abury's turn and he chose Melissa Downing, who was generally considered to be the second-prettiest girl after Wendy. The cat-calls were fewer and quieter this time, as they too sat down together and the next few selections were made with less embarrassment and increasing bravado. At one point, Kathryn Taylor raised her hand and asked why the girls didn't get to choose, but Mrs Tipps just rolled her eyes and told the lessening line of boys to continue. I was glad the girls didn't get to choose because I imagined none of them would want to choose me. It would've been like the times I got picked last in football, only far, far worse.

We were down to three boys: Thomas Nelson, Martin and me. It was only then that I realised that only one girl – Patricia Bunting – was left. Patricia was short and wore glasses and had an inability to button her cardigan evenly. Thomas spoke her name in an over-bored drawl that drew a laugh from the seated boys. Patricia's response was a look of accustomed resignation, as if this was how things had always been. They took their seats and I stared at the back wall, wondering what was going to happen next.

Mrs Tipps broke into my thoughts, "You there," – she was talking to Martin – "your turn now. Come along, make your choice."

We looked at her.

"But there's no girls left," said Martin.

She coughed loudly, without covering her mouth, and spray moistened the hair of Joseph and Wendy.

"There *are* no girls left," she said. "But there is *someone* left, isn't there?"

Martin turned to me slowly.

"But he's a boy!"

"Full marks for observation," she commented as the class giggled nervously, "Now hurry up."

Martin protested as I observed the proceedings with a vague sort of wonder but Mrs Tipps was having none of it. In the end he called my name stubbornly and we took our seats to a chorus of whoops and whistles. My face was burning. I looked straight ahead.

Mrs Tipps stood in front of us. She looked pleased with herself.

"Thank you for indulging me children. You may take from this experience what you will. When we resume our studies in the afternoon, you will return to where you are sitting now. Indeed, this will remain the seating plan until I am no longer your teacher."

There was an outburst of protests which ended when she slammed the blackboard duster onto Joseph Arbour's desk, sending up a plume of chalk. There were five minutes left until the lunch bell rang, which we were ordered to spend in Quiet Contemplation. I contemplated Mrs Tipps's last few words, wondered again what was wrong with Miss Maughan and if she would ever come back at all.

†

Martin and I ate our lunches at the tables set aside for the handful of children who didn't have school meals. Patricia Bunting sat opposite us, but she talked even when she ate, so we ignored her. Afterwards, we spent the rest of the break walking round the perimeter of the yard together, ignoring the sniggers and whistles that came whenever we passed people in our class.

·

†

The afternoon period was given over to our ongoing history project. Mrs Tipps was waiting for us when we got back and she stood expectantly as we took our new seats.

"Well children, I understand that you have been learning about the Ancient Greeks these last few weeks. I can assume then, that you are all capable of continuing this particular topic with the minimum of supervision."

Kathryn Taylor raised her hand again.

"Miss Maughan usually has us watch a programme that she records for us each week. She keeps it in her top drawer. She–"

"Television is for the home at best young lady. In *my* classroom, we *read*."

She stared at Kathryn hard and then began tossing out the withered old textbooks that we had been studying from, each one landing accurately and with a clean *whump!* on our desks. Her final words uttered, she sat at her desk and, with her eyes, dared us to speak. We opened our books.

†

The three o' clock bell couldn't come soon enough and Martin and I made our way to the gym. Mr Arthurs wasn't anywhere we could see so we went straight to the equipment cupboard. We leaned over the open casement where hockey sticks, badminton rackets and other assorted items were kept and I cleared away a corner, pointing out the cluster of tiny black creatures hidden there.

"That's not an ant nest," Martin said. "Ant nests

are piles of dirt with a hole at the top where they go in and out. This is just... These are just ants."

I stood deflated.

"But they're pretty good all the same," he offered.

We leaned over together, watching the ants as they filtered in and out of a tiny crack in the tiled floor. Martin spoke first.

"I don't like Mrs Tipps."

"I don't like her either."

"What was that about earlier? The experiment-thing and moving us about."

I nodded. "Miss Maughan wouldn't have done that. She would've let us sit where we wanted to."

"Do you think we should do something? Tell someone?"

I began to say "Who–" but there came the squeak of footsteps behind us and Mr Arthurs stood at the door, sweating and wheezing gently.

"Sorry sir. We were–" I hesitated. "We weren't doing anything."

He laughed. "I don't doubt it. Still, I couldn't help overhearing. Has something happened? You know you boys can always talk to me."

It was true. Mr Arthurs gave the annual Stranger Danger talk every year, telling us that we must inform an adult immediately if we ever saw any men we didn't know around the school or if anyone ever offered us a lift home. I remember seeing the staff list on a rare visit to Mr Dalton's office. Mr Arthurs' name was followed by the words *Physical Education & Pastoral Care*. I didn't know what that meant at the time but it had the word care in it and I knew that Mr Arthurs took Communion to those people who couldn't get to church.

The boys were always told that they could talk to Mr Arthurs about anything they couldn't talk to another person about; the girls, Miss Maughan, but I'd never approached Mr Arthurs about anything on account of his strong and personal odour. This was different however, because he was approaching us and I wanted to know why what had happened had happened. I wasn't able, back then, to articulate it, but I felt that I – that we – had been treated in a not-right way by a teacher, and as much as I didn't think that it was okay, neither did I think I could do anything about it. I looked at Martin, willing him to speak.

"Well sir, something did happen before and we don't know what to do."

Martin related everything that had happened that day, including the bit about Current Events and even his own story. As he listened, Mr Arthurs had one hand in his tracksuit pocket. He was rubbing himself gently. Martin finished speaking and there was a dense silence between the three of us until Mr Arthurs took his hand out of his pocket and looked at us both, breathing slowly through his nose.

"Well, it sounds like it's been a funny day for the both of you. I wouldn't worry about it too much though. These sorts of things usually have a way of fixing themselves without you even knowing."

He leaned forward, his large hands gripping the edge of the box on which he rested.

"You'd better be off home. I should be closing up."

Martin and I left the gym. Our shoes scuffed the buffed floor, echoing around the room. Once outside, we walked in silence across the fields. I began to speak, but before I could, Martin slugged me in the stomach and I fell to the ground.

He ran away, towards the gap in the fence. I lay still, tears threatening, my hands clutching where he had punched me, breathless, then sat up slowly until the pain subsided. I looked around, wondering if Mr Arthurs had seen any of what had happened, but he was nowhere, so I got up and made my way home.

†

When I got back, I crept upstairs to the bathroom and went to the toilet, expecting to see blood, but my water was just the deep yellow of a person who hasn't drank enough on a hot day. I was aware that I smelled strongly of sweat and, with the legacy of Mr Arthur's odour in mind, ran a bath. My mother's tired feet traipsed upstairs and she knocked on the door.

"Are you coming down to eat?"

"Soon," I said. "I'm hot. I just need a wash."

"Well don't be long," she said, as she inched down the stairs. "Your food will get cold."

I stripped down and slipped in. My stomach no longer hurt and I could feel the dirt peeling away from my skin as the water swirled around. I lay still until the water cooled and it became uncomfortable to stay in. It was the first time Martin and I had argued in all the time we'd known each other. It was also the first time anyone had ever punched me and it was this intent to hurt, more than anything, that was the worst thing.

Later, at the kitchen table, I thought about the whole day. I wanted to know what it was all about; why everyone had acted the way they had, began to wonder why anyone acted the way they did. I considered asking my mother about it, in some oblique way that didn't implicate anyone, but knew it was the kind of question that would lead to further, more complicated questions in return, ones which I wasn't ready to answer. The only person I could ask about it, I realised, the only person who I'd ever known to answer anything in a straight and simple way, was Miss Maughan, and again I wondered what was wrong with her and when she would return.

†

Her absence the next day was a disappointment. We filed in and Mrs Tipps made sure we sat in our new places. Martin was already in his seat and he looked at me, visibly ashamed. We began the day again with Current Events. I reported further on the person who had killed their own baby and informed the class it was believed they wouldn't go to prison because they were mentally incapacitated, which meant it wasn't their fault they did such a terrible thing because they didn't know what was right and what was wrong. This was how my mother had explained it when asked. I didn't hear the other contributions because I was thinking about other adults who might be mentally incapacitated and if such a thing might apply to certain of our teachers. I decided to ask Miss Maughan about it when she returned.

After Current Events was Maths, which I liked because I didn't have to raise my hand to ask questions, something I always seemed to have to do with other subjects. While I had my head bowed over a series of sums, Martin slipped me a note that read *Sorry about yesterday. Still friends?*

Mrs Tipps loomed. She peeled the note from me and made a great show of striding to the front of the classroom, where she read the contents aloud in a childish voice. As she spoke, adding flourishes for comic effect, I stared past her and at the desk, where Miss Maughan's flowers were turning brown. The class burst out laughing and she didn't call for silence. I lowered my head and continued with my work until the bell rang and everyone else – Mrs Tipps included – had left.

During the second half of the morning I kept a low profile. I tried to talk to Martin in the lunch break but he walked away. I was standing on my own when Wendy Bayham came over. Her friends stood a little way off, looking at us. She spoke first.

"She's funny, Mrs Tipps."

"I don't think so."

"No, I mean funny-*weird*, don't you think? I do at least."

I looked at her cautiously, "She is, yeah."

"And that thing yesterday, splitting us all up. And you and Martin. That was just stupid."

I smiled, cautiously.

There was a silence then, and I asked, "When do you think Miss Maughan will come back?"

"I don't know," Wendy said. "Soon, I hope."

We stood there, not talking again for moments that seemed longer than they were, and then she invited me to join her friends. We sat on the grass until the bell rang and I didn't speak, but stared at the ground and dug my fingers into the dirt.

†

Wednesday afternoons were given over entirely to physical education. There were no changing areas, so we had to get ready in the cloakrooms; really a series of wooden partitions outside the gym, with the boys on one side and the girls on the other. I undressed, hesitantly, away from everyone else and waited until they had gone into the gym before following.

Mr Arthurs had gotten everybody started on warm-ups. Patricia Bunting sat on a bench, in uniform because she never did physical education, being in possession of a series of mysterious notes that always seemed to excuse her. She acknowledged me with a smile before returning to the book in her lap. Mr Arthurs wheezed at me to join the rest of the group, who were taking it in turns to leap over the pommel horse.

I began a half-hearted jog, increasing in speed as I neared it. Just as I placed my hands upon the handles there came a sharp wolf-whistle. One arm gave way and I fell back onto the mat, not even making it to the other side. There was an explosion of laughter – laughter occurred everywhere around me lately, it seemed – that echoed about the gym.

Mr Arthurs just shook his head. Instead of re-joining the queue, I ran out and into the cloakrooms. After getting changed, I made my way to the secretary's office. Mrs Galsworthy peered over her glasses at me with suspicion, the only look I believe she possessed.

"Please…" I began, "I don't feel well."

I made a point of touching my stomach gingerly. Mrs Galsworthy's eyes narrowed.

"I see," she said, in a tone that suggested that she didn't. "In what way don't you feel well?"

"I just feel…" I paused for effect, "…sick. I fell over in the gym and think I hurt something."

"It's nearly two o' clock," she said, "Can't you wait another hour?" But I allowed one of my arms to hang loose, twisted my face and she relented.

I lay on the couch with a blanket. My mother had collected me from school and was too busy with everything else that made up her day to be too concerned, beyond making sure I didn't need a doctor. Nor was my father overly interested in why I was horizontal all evening beyond establishing certain baselines regarding my immediate health.

The next morning my mother felt my forehead and regarded me sceptically but allowed the absence. By the end of the afternoon I'd made a full recovery. The weekend droned by – albeit without the usual calls from Martin – and when Monday came I felt less anxious about returning to school.

†

I was late and the classroom was quiet when I entered. Everyone was in the seats Mrs Tipps had moved us to but she wasn't there. There was no-one at the desk but I knew Miss Maughan hadn't returned because the wildflowers in the vase were dead. At the back of the room stood Mr Dalton. He waited for me to take my seat, then strode to the front of the room. I pulled in my chair and looked at Martin but his face was firmly forward. Mr Dalton began to speak.

"Good morning. I am sorry to have to inform you, but Miss Maughan will not be returning. Nor will Mrs Tipps. In the absence of a suitable replacement, I will be taking your class for the foreseeable future. We will begin the morning with a spelling test."

With a quiet solemnity, we did as we were told. The day passed slowly, as did all our days the rest of that year with Mr Dalton. Life at school and at home continued much as it always did. I didn't tell anyone about what happened in the gym cupboard – I suppose Martin didn't either; we never were friends again – and Mr Arthurs retired a few years later anyway.

We also never found out what happened to Miss Maughan; no-one seemed to know anything. After a while she became a memory, one in a series of people who had been in our lives, but then became so no longer. After the end of that first full week with Mr Dalton I emptied the vase with its dirty water and its dead wildflowers and put it in the cupboard at the back of the room where it remained for the rest of my time there; empty, unused and forgotten.

Ursula Brunetti

Satellites

After school Harley sits next to me on the bus. The fact of someone entering my space takes me by surprise. It makes me look right at him. "You all right?"

I tend not to look at people's eyes because I don't want mine to be seen. My brother Jay used to say my eyes "gave everything away," and I don't want to do that. I want to keep everything inside, give nothing away at all. Nevertheless, I look.

"You like going on top then?" Harley says, that first time he sits down. He sets the tone without me knowing – I always ride top deck. We take a corner. My stomach swerves.

"I suppose," I say and Harley laughs to himself, chews gum, flashing me a piece. I see it roll like a false pearl between his teeth. Soon the air between us is clotted with spearmint.

It's clear Harley is older than me, but I am only fourteen and most people are. His eyes are the colour of paving stones. His skin is sunless. His hair as colourless as tap water when it falls from the faucet. I notice a brown mole on his cheek, raised and furred like a square of velvet that doesn't belong.

"Want a bit?" he says, offering me a foil rectangle. I open it and place it in my mouth, where I can feel my heartbeat pushing into my teeth.

"What's your name then?" he says.

"Dalia," I say, chewing. My tongue cools with the flavour of the gum and bowls it into a ball. When I realise what I have done I take it out and press it into the foil. Wrap it carefully. Squash it flat.

"I'm Harley," he says, "You don't mind me sitting here do you? What's your stop?" I shake my head. I can't think what my stop is called, only that when it arrives, I always ring the bell, that the bus always stops, that I always get off. I realise I don't know where the bus goes once it rattles past my house.

"The next one," I say and Harley nods.

I watch him in the reflection of the window. He has sparse stubble on his face that he is proud of. Every so often his hand moves over the bristling stripe of flesh beneath his nose, his burred cheeks and over his chin. Occasionally it swoops around the back of his skull in a deliberate movement, the way you might spin a globe. The movements are habitual and I find myself wondering what each surface feels like. Something about him reminds me of Jay. After five minutes of nothing, I realise it's the way he owns the silence as though it's a channel he can choose to tune into. He puts his feet up on the front window and I immediately look away. His hand grazes mine and I wonder what he knows about me and why he has chosen to sit with me. Word gets around in small places. His fingers flex and I feel like a drop of liquid rushing toward a plughole, unable to change direction.

I get home. The radio is on and dad is in the kitchen staring into the centre of the table. His shoulders move in acknowledgement as I come through the door.

"What you doing here?" I ask. He should be at the high school, the one I don't go to.

"I wasn't feeling great," he says. He looks weighted down, sunken. As normal.

"How was school?" he asks. I tell him we had physics. His subject.

"Oh yeah?" he likes to know how the other schools teach. His school is failing and mine is not. I tell him Mr Sanders spoke about trajectories and balanced and unbalanced forces. He likes to know I've been listening, that I can be present, somewhere.

"Ah yes," he says, as though reminding himself, "trajectories – masses in motion that follow a path as a function of time."

"Something like that," I say, searching the cupboards for snacks, "reckon you could help me with my homework?"

"I'll look later," he says, his voice weary, cracking with static, "right now, I'm going to lie down."

He leaves the room and I go to binge on TV. Two months ago the Sky man installed a satellite dish at ours. "Somewhere discrete," mum had asked, like she didn't want people to know we craved entertainment, that we needed an excess of distraction.

There are infinite shows about neighbours, families and friends, simulations of real life. Even The Simpsons with their dysfunctional dynamics, Bart and Lisa revolving as opposite heroes. I can't watch this kind of thing anymore. I press repeatedly on the remote until I find something neutral – something with no points of reference. Eventually I opt for a cartoon, Futurama – where nothing is real, or true, or pretending to be.

Harley starts to join me regularly, wearing his sports jacket that is lined with plastic. It holds the scent of deodorant and unwashed laundry. It makes me think of the boys changing room at school and Jay's old sports kit. We usually take the two front seats, top deck. Sometimes Harley talks and I listen.

He tells me about retaking his A-levels, his job stacking supermarket shelves, the Nikes he is saving for, his favourite Eminem songs. Sometimes he lays his arm along the back of the seat so that I can feel his jacket on my neck. The movement sends blood rushing round my body. This is the way danger feels. A surge of heat. A misplaced pulse. He says he is nineteen in June, that this shit is temporary. That he wrote off his car. That he can actually drive.

"One day," he says winking, "I'll take you for a spin."

Sometimes we share earphones, listen to his Walkman.

"Hear this, such a tune," he says. His eyes hover around my neck.

The lyrics are violent and angry, shouted over a beat that trips over itself and restarts. Harley nods his head, closes his lids. I don't understand the words but I like being chosen to hear them. Sometimes I feel angry and violent too and I wonder if Harley knows this, whether I have given that away in the slip of my eyes.

As the rapper barks about 'minimum wage pay cheques' and 'maximum rage disrespect' Harley's head bops and I window watch. From above, the world seems smaller, the people and places less significant. I have an aerial view over hedges. I can glimpse the inside of bedrooms, the contents of conservatories and I wonder if people have died in these benign-looking places, next to the flowerbeds or in front of sun-bleached swings. In the gardens that fly past I look for discarded balls and when I see them I wonder if Jay has somehow put them there for me to find. I know thinking like this is childish, but technically I am still a child. When it's my stop Harley presses the bell for me.

"See you tomorrow," he says. I look at his eyes. Over time I have become less afraid of what he'll see in mine. Sometimes I want him to look more closely, to see what's missing.

Dad helps me with my homework. I have a worksheet with simplistic illustrations that depict planet earth and a satellite travelling along a circular dotted line.

He explains, "Celestial bodies – like satellites in this example, they travel at the same rate as the earth, fixing them to a point, making them 'geostationary.' So their trajectories are fixed – they orbit at a constant distance."

He is holding an apple and a clementine to demonstrate. In the piss yellow glare of the kitchen light I notice his scalp shining through his hair. For the first time I become aware of how he will look as an elderly man. The cheeks sagging, the eyes hollowed. Life's questions cut into the skin. He is almost there.

"So they're moving but not moving?" I ask, confused. I find it hard to concentrate but I want to please him – to make my existence worthwhile.

"Well," he says, satisfied I'm participating, "let's put it this way, because they are traveling at the same speed that we're traveling at, they *appear* as though they're not moving at all."

"So it's an illusion?" I conclude. I take the fruit out of his hands and roll them across the table. He catches the clementine. The apple falls.

"Exactly," he says. Dad can only talk to me about physics. Anything else is too intimate. He asks tentatively about my understanding of forces and mass, hoping that if I can master their rules, it will explain how the world works so he doesn't have to. I prefer mum's take on it all. Sometimes I hear her say that nothing makes sense and that life is "inexplicably unfair."

In the evening dad and mum sit on opposite chairs in the lounge, dad with his marking, mum looking drawn, eyes fixed on a novel from her book club, but she never turns a page. From the kitchen, there is the constant hum of radio conversation. In the doorway I hesitate whether to join them and flick on the TV. I don't. I feel like a disturbance – an anomaly that doesn't belong. I bounce off their atmosphere and gravitate to my room. In bed I think of Harley and how much I'd like to run my hands through his hair. How the silence between us on the bus has a different charge altogether.

The next day on the way home, Harley is not on the bus. I ring the bell too early and it seems to take ages to stop. When I get in, the house is as I left it – tidy, clean but shrouded in shadows. The radio left on, as always. Outside of dad's help with physics, none of us at home can talk, but none of us can stand the silence.

Summer term and summer rain. The top deck thickens with olfactory grass stains and pheromone musk. My breasts have gone up a cup size. I clasp them in my hands at night and feel grateful to have something to hold while mum whimpers downstairs. Her voice is high-pitched. Reedy like a lost girl's. Her grief often comes out after rainfall, like her feelings have reached saturation point. She howls on days when the front door swells in its frame and the gate whines in the breeze. I hold my chest until her sobbing wanes. I count the days until the anniversary. The date looms at the end of the month, taking us all further away from the days when Jay was living.

A week later and the bus is taking Harley and I on its usual route.

"What's your number then?" Harley says.

It's an instruction, not a request. I've had a mobile phone for five whole days. My phone is heavy and manual and slow but it is also the most exciting possession I've ever owned. Modern and sleek with promise. I wish I could show it to Jay. Already I have composed Jay messages and sent them to random numbers using Jay's date of birth, or his date of death. On its small orange screen, messages appear from nowhere; transferring information specifically for me, usually from mum, "What time are you home?" or replies to my messages to Jay, "Who is this?" "Wrong number." "Message not delivered." Always the one-inch aerial points hopefully at the top, waiting to transmit.

I have spent evenings memorising my number. As soon as Harley asks, it emerges from my lips like a poem. Treble seven, double six, three, two, five... Harley punches it into his own industrial phone. Nervousness runs through me like spoiled milk, lumping and liquid.

"Like this we can keep in touch," he says, "I'm on study leave now – we should hang out."

Something twists through his gaze, like puddles disturbed by a temporary sunburst. I see it flare momentarily and I want to know what it means, this lifting of colour. "I'll text you," he says, "ok?"

It is Saturday, the day before Jay's anniversary. Mum and dad have planned a walk and a meal but I'd rather we treated it as just one more day. I have been checking my phone every few minutes for well over forty-eight hours. Nothing has come through. The hours expand. At eleven my phone finally beeps. It's Harley. He wants to see me. My nerves bend with gratitude. We are so different and I am too young but I want to fast forward for a while. Try being a future self. I text him back. I want to see him too.

"Where?"

I don't know where he lives, only that it is further, beyond. As I wait for his reply I roll deodorant under my armpits. I apply silver eye shadow and comb mascara on my lashes until they thicken, until my eyes are shielded, until I look like someone else. I desperately want to be older. To stop being Jay's sister for a while. To stop being a suburban legend.

Harley replies, "Bus stop. I'll meet you there at one – eight stops after yours."

The sky is clear but the sun's heat is weak. The air feels cool and uncommitted, as though it's just passing through this town, my limbs, this life. Harley is there at the end of the road, just down from his bus stop. He lives closer than I thought. He is wearing a baseball cap and all his clothes seem too large for his body. Mine on the other hand are too small. My skirt rides up as I walk. My top reaches across my stomach exposing a pale slice. My bra pinches my new breasts together and pushes them skyward. Everything is ascending.

Harley leads me down a road where wires criss-cross like black spaghetti above us and accumulate at wooden posts. We head into an estate where St George's flags hang in the windows, reminding me of British Red Cross charity appeals. People in crisis. The Top Forty booms from passing cars, their bass lines pounding and physical. As they speed past splitting the air, my heart stop-starts but I succeed in kicking the memories away.

He holds my hand as we pass squat houses whose satellite dishes point toward the heavens like chrome flowers. The dishes look expectant and stoic, ready to receive whatever is coming to them.

"This is me," he says. Harley stops outside a house where long grass is scattered with dandelions. There's a fence dividing his house from his neighbour's, the paint on it has cracked. Bins overflow with beer cans and I can see the pale moon of a football in the lawn, almost hidden from view with grass. I pretend not to see it. Even now, I wonder if Jay somehow placed it there and what it means if he did.

"Think everyone should be out," he says and I don't know if this is good or bad. I think of my family and the calcified ache that exists between mum and dad and me. Our shared suffering has a way of growing. Lengthening and deepening like an unwelcome after-taste. I decide it would be better if I never met Harley's family. Especially as Harley has a sad house and I have never thought of Harley as a sad person before. I don't have space for other people's pain and the realisation makes me feel tense, like coming was a bad idea.

When he opens the door, we're immediately in the living room. In the corner there is a heaped shape in an armchair. It is topped with copper coils. It creaks a little on the leather. Two glass circles flash with daylight from the open door.

"Oh, hi mum. Didn't think you were here," he says. Harley does not introduce me. She makes a noise that sounds entirely disinterested, as though she is merely existing, as though to communicate would be to admit to being a person, when perhaps she is not a person at all. From where I am standing, it is hard to tell. As my eyes adjust to the dim I see she is over-weight, that she wears her wounds on the outside. I can't see behind her glasses but I can see the mottled pink of her corned beef skin, the unkempt expanse of hair. She emits the same bleak atmospheric charge as my own mum. For a moment I wonder if she is my mum, transported into another body, into another living room, like the satellite images that get sent down from space.

We walk across the thick red carpet, which stretches across the small living room and up the stairs. It is three dimensional with dirt. Debris and crumbs have fused to the fibres, dog hairs are so embedded that in parts it looks grey. Harley looks back at me and his eyes are giving something away but I can't unscramble his signals. He remains elusive and I remain attracted to him; his nearly nineteen-ness and the way he has adapted to living in an unfeeling way that I have yet to master. We are heading to his room and I wonder if I should leave now and get the bus back home. Instead I keep going, matching each of his footsteps.

Inside Harley's room there is a slim cupboard, a single bed, football posters on the wall, a can of Lynx on the side. On the floor is an extra-large bottle of Cola, half empty. A television tops the drawers at an angle to his bed. It is already on. He skips through the channels using the remote.

"What d'ya fancy?" he says.

"I don't mind, whatever," I say, "nothing scary though. I don't like horror." He selects the movie channel and Toy Story bursts colourfully onto the screen. The volume is high. I can barely hear him speak.

"This ok?" he says, sitting next to me on the bed.

"I think I can handle this," I say and he smiles, waiting. We both know that I am here for something, except he knows what it is and I do not.

We watch the screen without talking. Harley suggests we get under the covers and I do what he says. The sky outside continues to show blue through his window and it strikes me that this is a waste of a day – to be inside watching a film I have seen many times. I think about dates on television and how there is sometimes a walk, a bowling alley, maybe an iced drink.

Conversation and compliments.

"Want some Coke?" he asks. I sip from the bottle. Flat air bloats inside my mouth before I swallow.

"Tastes weird," I say.

"It's got a bit of vodka in there. Not much," he says smiling, and swills it down his throat. I watch his Adam's apple rise and fall and it strikes me that he is a man. That I am a girl. I still have stuffed toys on my bed and some of Jay's too. For a moment I watch the screen; talking figurines chase each other into the road, and I realise it is barely four years since I watched this film with Jay at the cinema, the two of us stuffing our faces with sweets. It's barely three years since we spent that summer playing football in the front garden. Jay practicing his tackles, me showing off my long-distance kicks, the ball cutting a curve in the air, Jay bounding after it. Only two years since I spoke to the grief counsellor. Just over one year since I left middle school. I feel tired and slow – I should be older by now. I should be much further ahead. My head sinks into Harley's pillow. Tentatively I position my arm around his waist. The thought of having so much further to go makes me anxious. I already feel sore. I want to get it over with.

Harley screws the cap on the Coke, puts the bottle on the floor and starts toward me with his mouth. His breath is carbonated and stale and his short hair shines in the sun. It is the colour of ash – light and insubstantial. My pulse hammers through my veins and I think of the ashes being scattered on the beach, how they fell too fast, pulled wantonly toward the ground. I think of my foot kicking the ball too hard, sending it soaring in an extended arc. Jay's determined running. The noise of the car. The lingering, visceral silence.

Harley removes my knickers and pushes my skirt

up. The characters enlarge on the screen. A dinosaur. A cowboy. A slinky. An astronaut that wants to return to space. I think of satellites orbiting the planet in hushed isolation, sending the entertainment down to stop the act of thought. Harley's underwear is blue and green check – they remind me of something my dad would wear. I feel stunned and stiff. When I see that Harley is hard, my heart turns over in my chest. His body is as white as flour but his shaft is a violent purple, it looks angry and determined and it points accusingly at me, like I deserve what's coming. I think of uncooked meat and feel disgusted at its ugliness, its involuntary movements. It is making small consoling nods, agreeing with itself, as though satisfied with some inner observation. He positions himself on top of me and I draw a breath, hoping that this will work. That the path I have chosen will propel me forwards and get me to the end, a little quicker.

It doesn't hurt as much as I thought it would but then Harley rolls me over so that I am sitting on top of him and everything feels sharpened. I look down at his pale face. His eyes are closed and I realise I could be anyone, or no one, that maybe all I am is a warm place to forget.

My body feels remote, as though my mind is balanced far above and that down below my flesh is adjusting to Harley's fast-piercing movements. I reach for his shaved hair, gasping as he slots further inside. I run my hand across his head, acknowledging how each short strand repositions itself, immoveable, committing to its direction of growth. As I do so, Harley opens his eyes and yanks down my top.

Harley rocks beneath me, his body damp with smoky secretions and I feel a surge of sorrow and guilt about Jay lurch inside my chest and threaten to spill out of my mouth, but it could just be regret. This is not how this moment should happen. Nothing is as it should be. I think how single actions can change the course of everything else and I wonder what the outcome of this one will be.

For a moment I catch sight of my breasts in the domed television screen where an advert shows a boy playing football on the beach with his family. It cuts me off at the shoulders so I don't know what my eyes are about to give away when Harley pulls me toward him and whispers that he could tell from day one I was "a naughty girl," that I had a look about me, like I wanted to be ruined.

Carol Dines

Forgiveness

L ast year, after my wife's sister died of cancer, Sylvie started to worry about her own health. She lost thirty pounds, counting points in Weight Watchers and bicycling every day.

When I told her I was proud of her, she rolled her eyes. "You sound like my father."

"What's wrong with being proud of you?"

"I'm not doing it for you. I'm doing it for myself."

A year ago now we had that conversation, before her trip to Italy, before it happened. Since then, nothing feels honest, no silence empty enough, no apology sincere enough. After thirty-two years of marriage, that's what anger does, keeps us deciding what to bury.

Sometimes I almost break free and think we're fine, like falling in a dream and waking up. Today is one of those moments. I get the nomination after the first hour bell, a phone call from the Superintendent, and right away my first thought is, Call Sylvie. She'll be so proud of you.

I don't call her. I don't want her to know she's my first thought. I don't want to share my happiness with her. I wait until dinner. Sunset grazes the kitchen table, rattle and howl of wind caught between storm and real window, life trapped inside, and the knowledge that what's important isn't getting free. I stare at her sweater, frayed sleeves, hair falling free from its clip. "I got the nomination, Principal of the year."

She turns, eyes bright and happy for me, but right away, I add, "I don't think I'm going to accept it."

Later she leaves a glass of warm milk by the bed, nutmeg and honey settling on the bottom. She claims it will help me sleep, another home remedy, something else to demonstrate she's trying. As I drink it down, I listen to the shower go on and off, reminding myself she's a good person – she saves water.

The door opens, and she climbs into bed, wet hair falling over her shoulders, skin greased, shapeless maroon pajamas. "Principal of the Year! Such an honor to be nominated." She burrows under blankets, her foot searching for warmth along my leg. "Think of the recognition for your school." The bedroom is cold because she likes the window open; air circulation she says, though it requires additional blankets to keep warm, a certain weight on top for her to sleep well. She wriggles her cold hand under my pajama sleeve.

I squeeze my arm down hard, harder than I need to. "You're cold."

"Proud, proud, proud," she says in the sing-songy way she did years ago when the kids brought home *A*'s and *B*'s on report cards. She strokes my arm. "You've worked so hard, and it's a far better school for your efforts."

I don't care about the nomination, and I wonder if not caring is a way of protecting myself. I feel old, suspicious of recognition and people who receive it. I might die soon. My mother died at fifty, my father at sixty-two. I imagine the intercom first hour. "We have some very sad news. Principal Jaffrey died in his sleep last night." Students I've suspended would cheer. How many teachers would come to my funeral? Five maybe, if they could get paid leave. The lunchroom staff would get a card and sign it, sending carnations in school colors, orange and blue.

"Who else was nominated?" Sylvie asks.

"Mitch."

"Mitchell West?" Her laughter falls like running water. "He's always running his tongue over his lips. I find him creepy."

"He gets more students into colleges than any other high school."

"An arts magnet," she says. "They can go to Ashland Pottery Institute and say they're going to college."

"He's good at fundraising." I stretch my legs under the covers. "I'm tired. I want to retire before I'm too old to enjoy life."

"You're only fifty-three," Sylvie says. "What if Minnesota reduces pensions like Wisconsin?" She moves closer, her breath smelling of toothpaste. "Most people would be thrilled to be nominated."

Rising to take a *Xanax*, pills my doctor prescribes cautiously, allowing only six a month, I take one and stare at my reflection in the mirror –my father's hooded eyes, slaggy cheeks, thin *English* lips. Sylvie used to tease me, "You've got the Queen's lips."

Before her trip last summer, we always rolled toward the center of the bed and held each other. Now I call to Kafka, "Come on, boy," and the dog jumps on the bed between us, sinks his weight along my leg.

Sylvie reaches across the dog, finds my wrist. "If you really want to retire, then retire. Just make sure you're doing it for the right reasons."

Uncertainty is its own undoing. What I can't forgive, even now, are all the beliefs that fell away, including my own worthiness. The ceiling has opened to sky, and the sky belongs to her. I don't want sky, don't want a wide expanse revealing my own narrowness – am I narrow?

She squeezes my wrist. "Please don't do this."

"What?" My voice a steep drop.

"Don't let what happened between us ruin it. You deserve the award."

I wait for the Xanax to take effect, thoughts slackening like flags on windless days. I wonder why the nomination feels like a burden, something else to dread.

I listen to branches break outside the window, ash trees casting off dead wood with each gust of hard wind.

Nine months ago, her first night back from Italy, I brought home take-out, calling first to ask what she wanted.

"Pad Thai, no tofu." That's what she'd asked for, and that's what they gave me, except I'd forgotten to say, "No baby corn either."

"Thirty-two years of marriage," she stared at the baby corn in her Pad Thai. "I've never eaten baby corn."

I glanced up, noticing the force of her voice.

We were sitting at the kitchen table, bank of windows overlooking the back yard, *Tithonia* thick with orange blooms, birds loud, ignorant of tragedy. This time of day, as dusk began to fall earlier, the sun fell through the windows, giving the kitchen a soft light. The sky was orange above the trees. We ate in shadow, preferring the gradual ebb of natural light to brighter LED bulbs above the table.

She picked out the baby corn. Normally she ate fast. I'd always found her eating habits masculine, the way she relished food. Big German fingers that helped push food onto her fork or chopsticks, oily lips, unself-conscious appetite. That was one of the things I'd had to stop noticing, her greedy eating habits.

She barely ate, and I apologized twice for the baby corn. She stirred the rice, looking at her plate.

"What was the theme this year?" I asked about the Italian school where she did her research.

Sylvie took a long sip of Pilsner, her throat gulping before she set down the bottle. "They designed all kinds of ways to study water."

An education professor at Augsburg, she took

student groups every summer to spend a month in Reggio Emilia, a communist area in northern Italy known for its progressive schools. Sylvie was writing her second book on learning environments.

"They built a water slide from the tree house," she explained, "and they analyzed puddles for organisms. Then they turned the slide into a water wheel that produced energy." She took a small bite of rice. "Then they wrote a play about the future of water and put it on for the community." Her somber tone didn't match her praise. Usually she bubbled forth.

"Was the biking hard?" I asked.

This year she'd stayed on an extra two weeks for a *BiciSole* bike tour through the Dolomites. She picked at her food. "Not that hard. Scenery was beautiful."

I'd just dished out my second helping of green curry with shrimp when I noticed her eyes filling with tears.

"I have something to tell you."

I sensed her reluctance and knew right away, by her silence, by the way her chin dimpled and lips tucked, something bad had happened. "Did someone do something to you?"

My worry made her flinch. "No, no, not that." She set down her chopsticks and reached across the table, held my wrist. "You and I, we're in this life together, and I know that." Her voice trembled. "So please try to listen and understand. I made a terrible mistake." She stared at the table. "I met someone."

My chest was full of wind, wind blowing hills of sand, burying whatever was there before. I breathed deeply, consciously expanding my belly, trying to absorb her meaning. I pushed aside containers of food, shrimp glistening like tree ornaments. I stood up, dumped my shrimp curry and rice in the compost bin. Afterward, I couldn't eat shrimp again. It tasted like murky water.

That night I walked Kafka after dinner, circling the block, stopping to look at our small bungalow on the corner, lights in upper windows where Sylvie was unpacking. Thirty years we'd lived there, raising two children in that house. She'd pulled the curtains closed in our bedroom. I stared at the other houses on our block and wondered if our neighbors were happy, televisions flickering behind shades. My eyes kept going back to our house, shock falling through me like rain in headlights. I thought of the staircase I'd sanded while she was gone, the yard I'd mowed, the rhubarb I'd picked and had frozen in baggies so she could make rhubarb bread. So many entrances to the future, and I wanted to block them all.

Back from my walk, I fed Kafka a biscuit, then took the stairs two at a time, finding her bent over her desk sorting mail. "Show me a photo. I need to see him."

"I erased them," her voice hoarse from crying.

I stood beside her desk, shoulders casting a shadow over the papers she was organizing. "Give me your phone."

She looked away as I scrolled photos. She actually had erased them, except for one group photo at the end of the trip. I recognized Marco right away, standing beside Sylvie. His face was deeply tanned, a wide smile, sporty sunglasses resting on his shaved head.

I thought seeing the photo would make him real, would give my anger a surface to stand on. I thought proof would settle my thoughts into a single outrage. "Is he married?"

"He doesn't believe in marriage." She looked past me, at the window, as if it were easier to see me through a reflection.

"No kids?"

"No." Her voice sounded tired, and yet I could also hear a flickering underneath, a spark not yet extinguished, and it made me feel ill. "I need to know everything. I deserve to know."

All that night, and for days and weeks after, I asked questions, as if there were a way to uproot the betrayal, pull it out by the roots, shake off the dirt and boil it into some kind of wisdom. Did he sleep naked? How did he touch you? What did you talk about? On and on, I kept returning to the same questions, until finally she admitted, "It was his smell. From the moment we met, it overwhelmed me, almost a chemical reaction."

"What kind of smell?"

"A body smell." She shrugged, staring me in the eye. "Like animal pheromones. I can't explain it better."

"You risked us," I waved my hand at the photos of our children on the dresser. "You risked all of this for a smell?"

Every conversation made me angrier. "What did you tell other people on the tour? Could Judy or Gordie find out?"

"No one knew. He'd be fired from the company if they found out."

I considered reporting him. After that night I began changing into my pajamas in the bathroom, self-conscious about moles, fleshy waist, my bald spot, the spot she used to rub at night in bed, tickling my exposed scalp. "Neanderthal." She'd keep rubbing, "Wolfie." Rubbing more, "Turtle," all the nicknames she had for me.

Months have passed, almost a year. We are separate, and I grieve the separateness, shadows living in the same house, shedding all but the necessary – fold, rinse, when will you be home?

She says something like, "Think we should hire Zanelli's again? They didn't come after the last big snow."

And I think how easy it is to disappoint her. "They've cleared our driveway for years. Zanelli's a nice guy."

We bought Roku, needing a way to spend time together.

She'll say, "How about a comedy, something light," and I'll say, "I'm in the mood for a thriller," and she'll say, "I'm tired of watching women die," and I'll say, "Men die too. In fact men die sooner." She'll pause, "In the last three shows, women have been murdered."

She's right. I can't argue.

And then she gathers her knitting and says, "You go ahead. I don't care about watching."

And again I feel abandoned, and again I say, "When did you start wanting something else?"

At the beginning, she sits back down. She owes me that. "I don't want to fight anymore."

"You thought you could get away with it." I make her say it.

"I thought I could have a separate experience without hurting you." Tears roll down her cheeks. "But when I got home, I couldn't lie to you."

"You can cheat on me, but not lie?"

"Lying would've been worse, between us forever."

Part of me understands, but understanding fuels a different anger. – She has taken control of deciding what to tell me.

Saturday morning, I wake thinking of the nomination. I have the weekend to decide before Monday, when nominations will be sent to the committee. I suspect I am the compromise candidate, no one's first choice, no one disliking me enough to argue against me either, the only reason I might actually win.

I smell bacon. One would think breaking a spouse's trust would somehow modify a couple's routine, but not in our case. We still have a big breakfast on Saturdays, dividing sections of the *Times*. She takes the main section, and I wade through the *Sports*.

Sylvie has been up since six, has already taken Kafka around the lake for a walk. The fan is loud above the burners, and Kafka is standing behind her, nose lifted toward bacon draining on a paper towel.

"Before you decide about the nomination, you should talk to someone." Sylvie cracks an egg. "I don't want you to make a mistake you'll regret." For years she's been encouraging me to make friends, going so far as to list possible candidates.

"I talk to you." I sip coffee and drizzle honey on toast, listening for what's behind her silence, wooden spoon tapping the bowl, slippers sliding across the wood floor, sighs full of measured air.

"Yes, but you're angry at me." She hands me a wet napkin to clean honey off the table, then nods at my fingers. She hates when I leave honey marks on the newspaper and the pages stick. "Maybe you should call Alex." Alex is a former teacher who's become a Buddhist monk. "He'd be a good listener."

I take a bite of toast, remembering when I was the more powerful one in the relationship, how power came from knowing what I wanted – marriage, two children, principal of an urban high school. Whereas it took her years to know what she wanted, whether to get pregnant, how many kids, whether to finish her Ph.D., apply for tenure track positions. She used to tell me *not knowing* had nothing to do with strength. "It actually takes strength not to know," she said. "*Not deciding* is different."

After she spoons eggs onto two plates, she hands me one. I sprinkle salt and pepper.

"That much salt?" She sits across from me, gives me a meaningful glance. "We all need someone to confide in. It's not good to hold everything inside."

"Do women count?"

"Sure."

"Michaela?"

"Kafka's dogwalker? You're going to tell her about your deepest fears?"

"I like her. We have good conversations."

"I know you do, but she's twenty-five. That's a little desperate."

"Is it?" I finish off my third piece of bacon. Add more salt to my eggs. Drizzle honey all over the toast without wiping my fingers.

There is a life in which my anger wins. Instinctive. More habit than I want.

Our daughter Judy knocks, pushes open the door, hands full with baby and diaper bag. "Do you have time to look at the stroller wheel, Dad?" She kicks off her shoes. "Front right wheel makes a terrible squeaking noise."

Sylvie takes the diaper bag from her arms. "Your father wants to retire early."

"Really," Judy hands me the baby. "Since when?"

I smell Kafka under the table, gassy in old age. Or it's the baby, resting on my lap. Judy looks like Sylvie, except she's grown rounder during her pregnancy. She has her mother's straight nose, dark eyes, frizzy brown hair pulled back behind her ears. "Nine month check-in yesterday," Judy beams at the baby drinking from her sippy cup. "Her head's in the ninety-eighth percentile."

"Takes after your father," Sylvie smiles. "He's been nominated for Principal of the Year."

"Dad, congratulations." Judy high-fives me, then leans over and takes the baby from my lap, kissing her cheeks. "Hear that, Sweetie? Your grandfather's the best Principal in the whole state."

"I'd rather retire." Standing, I zip my fleece vest, give my daughter a hug, kiss Emily on her forehead, and, glancing at Sylvie's scowl, head to the garage to see about the baby's carriage.

I like fixing things, taking things apart, putting them back together, an antidote for all the things that can't be fixed.

Unresolved anger will bury you, I tell my students. They smile back at me, eyes like asphalt under puddles. Sometimes I feel like a container, and the world is loose seeds shaking inside me. Someone has to take responsibility. Someone has to be the steady force sitting behind a desk when parents come to discuss their sons and daughters' behavior, posting Jimmy Tan's webbed toes in the shower, Mr. Sachs picking his nose at a red light, Mrs. Beltro's chemo wig askew during a fire drill. "Your daughter was texting and when the teacher asked for her phone, she stuck it down her shirt." Or, "Your son pushed a girl's face into the drinking fountain and she chipped a tooth. We do not tolerate this kind of behavior." I watch parents regard sons and daughters with a mixture of shock, recognition, and helplessness.

As I unscrew the wheel, I listen to Sylvie play *Patty-Cake* with the baby in the kitchen.

We haven't made love, not since it happened.

Twice she asked if we could "do our taxes," the phrase we used when the kids were young, and we locked the bedroom door and didn't want to be disturbed.

"Today would be a good day to do our taxes," she whispered one morning as I sat at the table reading the newspaper. Snow fell outside the window, and the kitchen was warm and smelled like toast.

But her kisses had changed, no longer pecks, but water drawn from a well.

She learned that from him, I thought, unwilling to live as a comparison in her mind. Her breath grazed the back of my neck. Instead of hugging her, I kept reading the newspaper.

Another afternoon, she got into bed next to me while I was trying to nap. She cupped my body from behind. Leaves rustled, and geese squawked overhead. Her hair smelled like oranges. I pretended to be asleep, and eventually we did nap until thunder woke us. "This is nice," she said, pressing her cheek to my shoulder blade. "I miss you."

I rose from the bed and left her there. My heart was full of old machinery, pistons and chains that refused to move. Mostly it was fear, that my body would make her miss him more.

Sylvie pushes the garage door open, and sunlight pours into the garage. "Judy's coming back later to get the stroller." She's dressed in leggings and fitted jacket, carrying a helmet under her arm. "Get a bike," she says. "Come with me."

"Hurts my back."

She pushes off, shoulders lowered over handlebars, wisps of brown hair floating behind her helmet.

Since last summer, she's evolved into a set of distances. She gave away her high heels. Lattes, instead of black coffee. Fingernails trimmed low, unpainted.

Buttermilk pancakes weekdays, which I don't mind, but she's always been so careful about carbs. Bicycling hundreds of miles every week, not like before just on weekends, but every day to and from work with bike lights and fluorescent jacket. Turmeric tea she drinks all day long. I smell it in cups even after she's rinsed them. "Aids digestion and inflammation," she tells me. "Helps my muscles after bicycling. You should try it."

Sunday afternoon Sylvie suggests we visit an art gallery. I know what she's doing, reviving our old ritual, all those winter afternoons during college when we'd go to gallery openings, drink free wine, and decide what we'd buy when we had money to spend on art. She's heard about an opening at *Intermedia Arts*, an exhibit composed of books on pedestals with nothing inside the covers, just blank pages. Visitors can write anything they want on the blank pages, and whatever they write is immediately projected onto a screen, a screen running continually, *twenty-four-seven*, hence the title of the exhibit.

The gallery is small, and apparently about to close. A sign says, *Moving! Pushed out by gentrification! Art never dies! It moves to the suburbs!* Inside, the room is packed with young people, many with wet hair, escaping the sporadic showers outside. I stare at illuminated walls. The movement of words gives me a headache. The crowd is young, girls with nose-rings and pink hair, boys in tight jeans and fitted jackets. The room smells of pizza from Galactica across the street. Instead of music, the sound system plays a heartbeat, and when it speeds up, the words fall faster, and when it slows, the words slow. I find it pretentious, words pouring down walls, words about saving wolves and organic apples and snowshoeing in winter and the tooth fairy.

I whisper to Sylvie, "This isn't art."

She frowns at me. "You're always angry at students for being on their phones. Well, here's a young artist trying to show what's happening to language."

"Young people make me feel old."

"Old people make me feel young." She moves to the pedestal next to us and begins writing. *I would do anything to go back in time and not make the same mistake.*

People reading turn and watch us. I lean over Sylvie's shoulder. "Stop it. Stop doing this right now."

She keeps writing. *You deserve the nomination, and you deserve to be Principal of the Year.*

I close the book, close it hard, slamming her hand inside it.

"Ouch." She lifts her hand and stares at me. Then she turns and heads to the coat rack. "I'll come back another time without you." She pulls on her coat, walks toward the door, fishing her pocket for car keys.

"I didn't mean to hurt your hand," I walk fast to catch up. "Don't overreact."

Opening the heavy glass door, she glares at me. "You've become a very negative person." She lets go of the door and keeps walking ahead until she reaches the car.

Sitting in the driver's seat, she doesn't turn on the engine. Her hands grip the steering wheel. "If you want to do this, you can."

"What am *I* doing?"

She stares straight ahead. "If you want to hate me, you can. And if you want to love me, you can. Either way can take on momentum. But just so you know? There's a moment when it stops being my fault, when what happened before isn't as big as what what's happening now." She turns and looks at me, shaking her head, tears welling in her eyes. "I don't know what you need to get past this, or if we even can get past it."

All these months, I've kept it buried deep, like an animal frozen to death in its own burrow. "I don't want you to go back to Italy."

She stares at me. "We've got ten students signed up. I need to finish this book to become a full professor." Her hands drop to her lap and she looks through the windows beginning to fog. "At some point, Liam, you need to decide if you can trust me. Otherwise what are we doing?"

Sunday nights the train passes through south Minneapolis, crossing the Cedar Lake Bridge. The horn wakes me, summoning me from sleep. I lie in the dark thinking of my father, how he never forgave my mother for her illness, complaining about her walker, its squeaky wheels, or worse, her canes tapping heavy arrhythmic footsteps as she moved up or down the stairs. So many interruptions, he told us, he had no choice but to renovate the garage into a studio where he did his engineering drawings, ate his turkey on rye, drank Scotch, and slept on a daybed, leaving us, his sons, to care for our mother after the aides went home. My older brother Teddy and I made excuses for our father. "He's finishing a project that's overdue." "He's behind again." But our mother refused to make us complicit in our father's neglect. "Your father has never been able to handle disappointment."

I miss my mother now, miss my chance to love her. But I also recognize I only felt this way after she died, when she stopped needing me. By the time I started high school, my mother had lost control of her bodily functions. Her fine angles had drawn sharp edges. Her eyes pulsed with vigilance, each movement demanding effort, as if her whole focus became strategic, how to get to the bathroom and back. Even then, sixteen years old, I felt my love for my mother had run out, and I didn't know how to make it come back.

Monday morning I can't find my car keys. Searching the top drawer of Sylvie's desk for her spare set, I find her second cell phone, T Mobile, clamshell phone. My body stiffens, every molecule recoiling from the surface of my skin. I press the large green icon, but the screen remains dead. I dig through the drawer, looking for a charger, but I can't find it. I think of taking it to Luke, the technology teacher at my school, to see if he can download whatever is there, love letters, texts, photos. I try calling Sylvie on our landline, anger pouring through me, and I'm immediately put through to her voice mail. I hang up. I leave the cell on top of her desk so she'll know I've found it. I grab her keys. I think about changing locks. Or packing my bag. Or taking Kafka and never letting her see him again. I need to walk.

Ten minutes later I'm at the dog park. Next to me sits a young woman, black hair curtaining her face, eyes hidden behind dark glasses, scrolling on her phone while her dog does its duty ten feet away. "Excuse me," I nod at the dog crouched behind the tree. "Isn't that your dog?"

She glances at me through dark lenses before returning her gaze to her phone, making no move to pick up her dog's poop. She is scrolling some site quickly, maybe *Tinder* or *Snapchat*, thumb moving with that repetitive slide I often see among students in the hallway.

"Pollutes the lakes, phosphates go into the water table," I tell her.

"Seriously?" Without raising her gaze, she mutters, "You need to chill."

Caught off guard by the strength of her voice, the authority of a woman so young, speaking to me, a fifty-three-year-old man, in such a hostile tone, I am taken aback. I stand and walk behind the tree, pick up the dog poop in one of my eco-bags, then place it on the seat next to her. "How hard is that?"

She sticks her phone in her purse and stands, walking away from the bench quickly, leaving her dog's poop bag behind. "Freak."

I pick it up and walk after her, the bag swinging slightly at my hip. "Excuse me!"

She glances behind, calling to her dog, "Cheerio, Come boy."

But Cheerio is sniffing Kafka, and I catch her dog by the collar, tossing the poop-bag to the ground near her feet. "Pick up the poop and throw it away like a decent person does."

The dog park encompasses two acres of field and woods, people sitting on benches and standing in groups. The young woman shouts, "Could someone please help me get my dog away from this guy?"

Two men start walking toward us as I hold Cheerio's collar. "All I'm asking is for her to pick up her dog poop," I call to the men. "Then she can have her dog."

The young woman, sensing protection in the men approaching, yells at me, "Who do you think you are, God of the dog park?"

Cheerio, hearing his master's shriek, wiggles free and runs to her. The girl laughs, "Come on boy," and leaves through the double chain link gate, tugging Cheerio's leash. "Asshole," she gives me the finger over the roof of her car.

I pick up the bag, throw it in the bin, and, sensing people watching me, feel both ashamed and justified, confused because of the anger roiling inside me. I face the two men who approach, throw up my arms, as if to claim my own innocence.

"Oh my God, have you seen what was posted?" Jan, my secretary, shows me the link on her phone, *High School Principal on Poop Crusade,* the *YouTube* video showing me chasing the girl, holding up a poop bag, screaming at her to put down her phone and take responsibility. "What were you thinking?" Jan whispers.

I don't remember yelling so loudly, but here I am, captured online, hundreds of students commenting:

God of the dogpark needs a muzzle.
Mr. J. loves picking up shit.
Hurray for Cheerio!
Leave Mr. Jaffrey alone. He's a good guy.

Six hundred *Likes* and counting. I head back into my office, Jan calling after me. "Sylvie wants you to call her office right away. She saw the video. She's called twice already."

"Tell her I have appointments."

The hallway buzzes with students replaying the video. I don't leave my office, not until I need my afternoon *Diet Coke* to stay awake. I go to the infirmary where I keep it in the refrigerator. The nurse comes Tuesdays and Thursdays and it is Monday, so I'm surprised to see a girl lying on the cot, reading a book. "Excuse me? Are you supposed to be here?"

Her short brown hair is shaved along one side, skin pocked, eyes caked with make-up. She turns her head toward me and smiles. "Are you going to chase me away too?"

I breathe deeply, nodding at her book. "That for a

class?"

"Humanities," she lifts the book, *Crime and Punishment,* so I can see the cover. "Have you read Dostoevsky?"

Her pronunciation is good which surprises me.

"Always meant to. Am I missing out?"

"Raskolnikov kills a prostitute to see if he can get away with it."

"And does he?"

"I'm not finished yet." She takes a bag of Doritos, squeezes it so that they break into smaller pieces, then tears open the bag, lifting it to offer me some.

"No thanks." I sit down on the cot across from her, coke in hand, not sure if I should leave. "Something up with your classes?"

"No."

"Family?"

"Can't I just stay here during lunch? I'm not bothering anyone."

"Mind if I listen?" I lie down on the second cot, thinking of the rule about leaving a door open, and instead I tell her, "Wake me if you hear footsteps," and then I say, "There was a Chinese King who had all the doors removed so he could hear his enemies approach." And then I add, "I've reached that stage."

She laughs. "You're funny."

Eyes closed, I nod. "Very few students realize that."

She begins reading aloud. I remember when Sylvie used to read to me in bed, and now, listening to the girl, my hands cover my heart. Beyond her voice I hear basketball balls dribbled in the gym, a coach's whistle. The team is playing Minnetonka Friday night, and already the whole school is gearing up.

When I wake the girl is gone, the phone ringing.

I'm expecting the call from the Superintendent, and right away I say, "Yes, I'm sure. It's time."

*

"Sylvie? Sylveeee!" I call out her name, then glance out the kitchen window. She's on the bench, sitting in her yellow slicker under a steady rain.

I want to forgive her. I'm tired of myself, as if I were born in a tight skin meant to hold everything intact, but instead it is holding me away from life, away from her, my heart lacking not what sinks but what rises.

I put on my slicker and rubber boots and join her on the bench. "Any reason in particular you're out here in the rain?"

"Rain is good for crying."

Geese fly over. Kafka sniffs the base of the bench. Congregations of darker clouds move stoically across the sky, thunder rolling in the distance.

I feel a sneeze coming on and dig into my pocket for a Kleenex, fingers going through a hole. I've been meaning to ask her to thread a needle. I sneeze twice, trying to hold it.

She hands me a Kleenex. "Don't hold it. You'll collapse a lung."

Her voice is so tender, so familiar, a nail pushed back into its hole after the picture is removed. "I didn't hide it from you," she tells me. "It's an Italian phone I got from the school. I left the charger in Italy. I thought I could use it when I go back. I didn't tell you because I didn't think it was important."

What's lost stays lost, but I don't tell her that.

"We can't go on like this." Her voice is hoarse from crying. She digs into her pocket for another

Kleenex and wipes her eyes. "If you want me to find my own apartment, I will."

There's no immortality in anger, no satisfaction.

The rain is loud, a curtain of sound.

"I could go with you this summer now that I'm retiring."

She takes my hand, holds it tight. The reach hurts my shoulder but I stay quiet, listening to the rain in its multitude of landings, flowerpots, rain-barrel, the long wooden fence.

Derek Dirckx

Dark in Here

Roy's house lies a half-mile past a dead end sign on a dirt road. The house itself is hidden from the road by a thick forest that's never been tamed, a lively mess of dancing green in the summer breeze. A plastic mailbox bearing only a four-digit number marks the beginning of a long driveway. Roy's is not the dead end. The road keeps going for I don't know how far. These details, among others, sort of make this the perfect place to be left alone.

The other details have less to do with location, and more to do with the property owner himself. For instance: his adult children live far away in other states with their own families; his wife died way back, and he's never dated since. Basically he's a quiet guy who keeps to himself, who never bought a cellphone, and who has lately been leaving his landline unplugged.

I am here in spite of these facts, a guest in Roy's home, sitting idly in the screened-in porch attached to the side of the house. Three of the walls in here are enormous windows, so my view is large and picture-esque. I see the long driveway coming through the trees to a clearing that is the yard. In the yard there is a dry bird fountain and seedless bird feeders. There are stone paths and empty flower beds all but buried in tall grass. A tire swing hangs from the branches of an ancient oak. Its rope is worn and disintegrating, unsafe for any child.

On the inside this porch reminds me of the hospital room where my younger brother died. It's probably the similar centerpieces: a very small bed with a chair on one side of it, and on the other, a stand with different drugs and accessories. There was also a wall-sized window in that room, but only one, overlooking a parking lot. So in other ways, of course, things were very different for Stevie. He had tubes leading out of him that connected to bags and beeping machines.

Stevie also had the luxury of doctors and nurses to stick needles in his arm, and to make sense of charts and display screens. Roy's not so lucky. He has only me.

Not to say we haven't had any help. The hospice nurse, who's nearing retirement age herself, helped a lot, which is either admirable or deplorable depending on your attitude. I've already forgotten her name. I had trouble focusing while she pointed at different blank prescription bottles and corresponding words she'd written on notebook pages. Roy thanked her more than once, and each time she muttered, "Lord knows it's your right, mister."

It makes me wonder what her motives must be, or where Roy happened to meet her in the first place. It's just a job to her, I suppose, the idea itself isn't quite so shocking. Folks often look to her for a grip on reality in the midst of their grief. She normalizes the frightening mystery by the sheer fact of her occupation. She's made a living of watching people die, and we didn't even ask of her that much.

Nobody offered me money to be in the room for Stevie's last breath. I doubt that would've changed my course of action, which was to find an unlocked janitor's closet down the hall where I could sit on the floor and shake and cry until an old gray man with a crooked back picked me up hours later. He was searching for a mop. He said, "Sorry, kid. This ain't the place for that."

Wherever that place might be, I still haven't found it. I thought that maybe it was here, at Roy's bedside, but now he hasn't woken up in two days and I'm losing confidence. The nurse hasn't come back, and I doubt she would if I called. It's hard for me to tell if Roy's actually breathing; his chest is so thin the blankets hardly rise. Beads of sickly perspiration appear first on the crown of his bald head, then accumulate in thin troughs of skin beside his mouth. I guess parts of him are still working. Every two hours I check for a pulse in his bone-thin wrist, hoping for a silence there that would excuse me.

The truth: I'm scared of who Roy will wake up to be if he ever wakes up again. I'm fighting the urge to abandon him. This urge grows with every hour that he's comatose. It'd be easy. I could take his car. I could plug in the landline, dial 911 and leave the phone off the hook. Then he'd be someone else's problem. But if I do that, what was the point of this? If I can't be here with him in the end, what have I learned?

In Minnesota everything dies once a year and then comes back to life. Some years the resurrection doesn't fully get underway until late May. This year was like that. It snowed on Mother's Day. That's how I keep reminding myself of when Stevie got sick. It was a few days after the last snowfall, weeks before the flowers got to bloom, when my brother stood up to leave geometry for the restroom. He made it halfway to the classroom door and collapsed between two rows of desks.

He apparently complained to my parents, days before of having trouble staying awake in class, but they didn't think much of it. What fifteen-year-old doesn't fall asleep in class? That poor math teacher must have felt quite out of her depth, especially when she saw blood leaking from Stevie's nose. Someone from the school office called an ambulance, and then my parents.

While my brother was being wheeled through the halls of St. Paul Children's, I was in my south Minneapolis apartment sleeping through a British Lit exam. The night before a bunch of us had gone downtown and acted as if we'd never get old- basically like children. It took me until five p.m. to wake up and arrive at the hospital. At that time the diagnosis was still unclear. The next day we met with a pediatric oncologist who said Stevie's type of leukemia infects the blood quickly, but in most cases responds well to treatment. "Very treatable," is what he said exactly. Low mortality rates. We believed him, because the alternative wasn't yet something we could believe.

They filled Stevie up with other people's blood every couple of days. They said it would save him, but I didn't see how he could live if he couldn't even make his own blood. They searched unsuccessfully through a database for possible marrow donors while a little more of my brother's life escaped him with every breath. The entire event was over in less than a week. As a loved one, you're expected to watch, even after the point is reached where nothing more can be done. Not that you, as a loved one, could ever really do anything in the first place, but eventually not even the people who are supposed to can do anything. It shouldn't surprise us, but it does.

Four hours before he died, I was there in the hospital room, sitting in the cushioned chair beside his bed. Mom was stuck on a loop. She'd hold her son's limp hand for a while, then the tears would well up and she'd shriek over the sound of machines barely keeping Stevie alive. Finally, she'd curl up in a ball on the linoleum floor and stay there for a half hour before returning to his side and starting the process again. Dad watched with his back against the wall. I stared through the only window in the room, a vast window taking up an entire wall. Outside was the top floor of a parking ramp. Mostly I saw cars, and people getting in and out of cars. They all moved slowly, dreadfully, no matter if they were coming or going.

I think my mother's depression resulted from her failing to find closure. Closure is something that you, as a loved one, gain by accepting certain facts and seeing them through to their natural ends. Not that I've found any, either. I folded like I was holding a shitty hand. I said, "I'm going to get some air," and I left.

After the kind janitor ushered me from his closet into the hallway and I made my way back to Stevie's room, he was gone, his body was, and the hospital linens had already been changed. Simple as that. I found Dad inconsolable in the waiting room. Mom had been handcuffed and dragged away somewhere for troubling the orderlies.

In the wake of Stevie's death, I thought I'd be able to help my parents remain intact if I moved into their home in Inver Grove for the summer. It felt like the right thing to do, anyways. Be there for the family. I spent aimless days not working, walking from one end of our tiny yard to the other, avoiding my mother until Dad came home. She never said, but I was certain she held it against me that I wasn't in the room. Her condition, the onset of which corresponded precisely with that phone call from the high school, accelerated rapidly once her youngest son passed away. She never even mentioned returning to work, never even sent an email. She floated through rooms cradling stuffed bears Stevie hadn't touched in ten years like they were infants. She wore nothing but shirts from his closet. Her gorgeous blonde hair, which had so far endured the stress of child rearing, inexplicably came out in soft clumps that followed her around the house.

We waited for her to be well enough to attend a funeral service, for her to prepare and deliver remarks, accept condolences. My brother's eulogy would've been brief. It would've been burdened with clichés about going too soon and God's plans. It never happened. In a tiny office furnished with a desk made from the same stuff as caskets, a stocky man in a black suit handed my father a marble urn. I came with him and had to hold the thing when Dad lost composure. Engraved on the front was STEVEN HUMBOLDT 2003-2018. The urn didn't bother me. Inside was only harmless ash, basically dirt.

Mom, on the other hand, became hard to look at. It was killing me, too, was what I told my father a week after the cremation in early June. Dad didn't protest. In fact, he offered to drive me to the transit center in St. Paul. He even paid for my bus ticket to Iowa City. A friend of mine went to school there, and had a spare room in his apartment for the summer. I honestly had no idea if I'd ever finish my English degree. Reading other people's accounts of life's tragedy used to thrill me, but after being in close proximity to true sorrow myself, important literature felt cheap and easy.

On the morning of my departure, a storm broke a sustained drought, setting new records across the Midwest for rain accumulation. Great sheets of water slid off the awning that covered the station platform. I could barely see the street. Maybe Dad was thinking of Stevie, too. The hospital was only a few blocks away. Maybe that's why he had no words for me. While the driver loaded bags into the belly of the bus, my father hugged me with a strength I didn't think he still possessed. I had no words for him, either.

From St. Paul the bus followed I-35 south through the suburbs, and after an hour all there was to see were muddy oceans of freshly tilled earth under a solid gray ceiling. Green dots formed neat rows across the fields. The crops got in late this year. It's peaceful country to drive through, even in the rain. It all looks so similar once you leave the cities, like you can be sure that some things will stay the same.

Inside the bus was far from crowded, yet somehow full of noise, mostly parents and their children. I tried to imagine what Iowa city would be like but could only conjure images of a modest high-rise surrounded on all sides by stalks of corn. The thought was so comfortably mundane that it put me to sleep almost immediately.

When I opened my eyes, the bus was parked at a truck stop that looked to be miles from anything. Except for the lanky driver slumped in his seat at the front, the bus was empty. Semis barreled up and down the interstate a hundred yards to my left. I had to take a piss, so I shimmied my way through the aisle and past the driver, who didn't appear to notice, or at least didn't care to open his eyes. He didn't look much older than me. I figured I had some time.

The rain had followed us to where ever we ended up. Still in Minnesota, I guessed after checking my phone. My clothes got soaked through as I sprinted from the bus to the front doors of the gas station. I didn't find any of my fellow passengers inside. The only person I noticed was a girl about my brother's age with purple hair and a nose ring, texting behind the counter. In my peripheral as I'd raced through the downpour, I had gleaned the dimensions of another building, some sort of fast food venue. Everyone else must have been hungry. A sign indicating the bathroom hung high on the wall near the back of the store.

After the bathroom I realized I was hungry myself, so I grabbed a bag of chips, a candy bar, a bottle of water, and brought it all to the counter. The girl with purple hair, holding her cellphone with two hands, ignored me for a minute and I didn't feel like bothering her.

It wasn't until we completed our transaction and I turned to open the glass door that I realized the bus was gone.

My first thought was to call my parents, but then I remembered everything at once, the whole preceding month, and realized I was stranded. Across the freeway, situated so as to be concealed by the bus before it pulled away, was what looked like a garage decorated with neon. I trudged slowly across the overpass, concentrating on the sound of water bouncing off the plastic bag in my hand, watching drops fall from the wet bangs in front of my eyes. As I got close, there were dents in the tan vinyl siding, and more neon displayed in front by the entrance. In bright red lettering, one of the signs said, HAPPY HOUR EVERY HOUR.

It was two-thirty in the afternoon when I walked in and seated myself at the first bar stool I encountered. I asked the bartender for a beer and a dry towel, then turned slightly to peer around the spacious room, which was basically empty on a week day. Someone sat a couple seats away, a man who'd been obviously staring at me since I walked in. Greasy hairs had been combed over to cover the embarrassing bald patches on top of his scalp. I caught his eyes, which were red with bags of pale skin hanging loosely beneath them. Every other feature of his face was somehow extenuated, sharpened to a point. His hands visibly shook. I counted four empty glasses in front of him, enough along with his appearance to give me the impression of a serious alcoholic. A sick dog, come here to die alone, curled up under the bar where he thought no one would notice.

He moved two seats closer. I could smell him, dry sweat and yeast. He said his name was Roy, and that he was drunk. Within twenty minutes he informed me of his other problem: a fast-growing tumor in his brain (glioblastomas), terminal, inoperable. He hadn't been back to the clinic for as long as Stevie had been dead.

"Jesus. I'm sorry, Roy."

"For what?"

"My brother just passed away," was the only thing I could think to say. He solemnly nodded, as if he'd already heard the news.

"My wife died in an accident many years ago," he said. "Sometimes I pray to her. I've never been religious, still ain't, but it's something I started doing. Sometimes I thank her for going the way she did, for not wasting anybody's time. She was like that, you know? She was always saying life's too short."

He stared at the wood grain through the bottom of a pint glass. He said, "People worry so much about dying. Well I'll tell you straight, it's worse being left behind."

Again, I apologized.

We ordered more drinks. Our conversation developed its own tenacious logic, something I grew more deeply implicated in the longer I sat and listened, nodding my wordless agreement to our hardships, as well as our half-realized solidarity. I harbored no delusions of making Roy's last moments joyful, or even comfortable. But I did believe he deserved better than meeting fate in the back of an ambulance leaving a bar. He said he couldn't bring himself to put a bullet in his head. He had too much pride to check out even a moment before the painful, gruesome end. If he stayed by himself, though, he'd wind up in a hospital, which was far more attention than he desired.

Roy's wife left him two children, a son and a daughter. Jesse did nonprofit work in the Columbus area, and Sarah was a stay-at-home mom in suburban Indiana. Roy had three grandchildren. He didn't get to see them nearly as often as he'd like, he told me. Money was pretty tight, even with the kids out of the house. Second and third mortgages had to be signed, and Roy had been working at a window factory up until his recent illness.

At one point he said, "I'm not going to tell them. I'm not going to tell anyone. I disconnected the phone."

He asked if I wanted to go with him to his house a few miles away. I said sure. He'd parked his baby blue pickup, chewed up with rust and stripping paint, along the side of the building next to a dumpster. We made it a few steps into the lot and Roy crumbled to the ground. I imagined an invisible ventriloquist hand had gotten bored and dropped his strings. The experience felt like a test. I stayed in control nicely, I thought later on. I slung his arm over my shoulder, slid him into the passenger seat, and removed the keys from his pocket. The tires spit bits of rock in the air that I heard ricochet off the glass door. The whole thing had a sense of urgency, like participating in a crime that I couldn't hope to fully comprehend.

We turned left, away from the overpass, then immediately a right on a dirt road. The steering wheel pulled from one side to the other, the tires drifting over the loose gravel. Roy slumped in his seat and vomited foamy bile all over his center console. Between dry heaves he instructed me to stay in the middle. I had never actually been on a road like this, but I didn't say that.

An intersection loomed ahead, with a yellow and black dead-end sign on the other side. Roy said to keep going straight and don't bother stopping, and soon the road banked down a slight hill. The truck's frame rattled badly when the tire caught a rut. The fields along the road suddenly sprung a thick network of trees and brush, engulfing us on either side, violently bursting with so much life the way things do the first week of June in southern Minnesota.

It wasn't until the morning after, when I woke up hungover on a couch in the living room, that I considered how absurd of a coincidence this was. I'd abandoned my own family in the hopes of shedding the weight of my brother's skinny ghost. Now I found myself surrounded by a host of strange faces that stared from every imaginable angle. In his lifetime Roy must have spent a modest fortune on developing photos and purchasing fancy artisan frames to display them in. The room felt familiar, hopeless, ugly.

The back of my skull touched the couch's bulky armrest. I watched the speckled ceiling, piecing together fragments of the night before. We'd spoken enough at the bar to provide context to the pictures. Or maybe the pictures validated the truth of everything Roy told me. My thoughts swam in unpleasant sensations, nothing was comfortable. I rolled myself over so that my chin perched on the armrest. Some of these people I assumed to be already deceased, like the woman who hung above the mantle in a two-foot-tall frame. She beamed with shining white teeth, beautiful and young, wearing a flowing white bridal veil. On the end table in front of my eyes was a vacation scene. Two teenagers, a boy and a girl with arms playfully outstretched, ironically pushing each other away, suggesting a familial relationship. Palm trees and breaking waves frozen in the background. They looked distracted, happy. The boy's floral print shirt was open to the wind. The girl's skirt of reeds fanned around her waist to reveal the polka-dot bottoms of her bathing suit. Her resemblance to the woman above the mantle was undeniable, and a sad thing to observe knowing what I knew.

I closed my eyes, wishing to slip back into unconsciousness, but my body wasn't having it. Somewhere in my bowels I sensed the need to get up from the couch, locate Roy's bathroom. What else would I come across, though? What other insights to this family's interior might I stumble upon? I didn't have to subject myself to it all at once. Best to ease into the reality of my situation the same way Mom quit smoking a few years ago. She started at a pack a day, then had one cigarette less each day until twenty days later she had her last. If I could pretend to be asleep for a few more hours, then maybe I'd be ready to witness the bathroom. A couple hours later, maybe I'd wake up Roy. After that, I had no clue. Gas moved itself around in my intestines and the urge to get off the couch subsided.

Of course, Mom picked the habit back up as soon as they let her leave the hospital after Stevie's death. She was inhaling two packs a day by the time I left. It didn't matter if I stayed with my parents or moved in with a complete stranger, I decided. Underneath me the couch cushions were damp. Sweat secreted from my temples and trickled into my ear. Part of me worried Roy had already died somewhere in the house, alone. If only it'd been that easy.

It didn't take me long to find him, or for him to find me. He tripped at the top of a staircase that emptied into a hall just off the living room. Tumors in his brain interrupted the normal firing of neurons, jumbling messages that should have been relayed to his appendages. His left foot had been giving him trouble, the most dramatic indicator yet of disease growing inside him. Ironically enough, it was his right foot that broke at the bottom of the stairs. He rolled screaming into the room I had been pretending to sleep in, and the reality of our situation washed over me like a sudden freezing rain.

Events proceeded far out of my control, from one unnerving moment to the next. I drug Roy across the hardwood floor to the porch, where he asked me to help him on to the twin bed that had recently been installed for this exact purpose. He'd planned on being confined to the ground floor. I then ran to the kitchen and found the phone, plugged it into the wall, and dialed a number Roy had scribbled on the back of his receipt from the bar. Nurse Delilah (I've just remembered) answered, sounding like she already knew me and had been anticipating my call. She showed up twenty minutes later with what looked like a big expensive purse. She wore normal clothes for a person her age, no uniform, with dark glasses shielding her eyes. The pictures on the walls seemed to interest her as much as the artwork hanging in a cheap hotel.

First thing, she plastered a small patch to Roy's lower back. After thirty minutes he quit making noise, and looked around the room unconcerned, waves of apathy lapping against the backs of his eyeballs. She said everything quietly, under her breath. There were requests, instructions, reminders. No time to think. The purse held a serious collection of drugs, whatever she could get her hands on, some useful and others perhaps too much so. I was given a sort of catalog in the form of hand-written notes. There was Valium and Lorazepam. Special eye drops that regulated the body's mucus production. Twenty and forty mg Oxycontin, along with some loose morphine tablets and fentanyl patches, one of which was already in use. The patches employed extended release technology, for the recurring days and nights of overwhelming chronic pain, unbearable pain, and for the eventual onset of dysphagia. Delilah said, "Use with extreme caution. No more than one per forty-eight hours." Then she told a story of a young woman, a coworker of hers apparently, who committed suicide with scraps clipped from patients' prescriptions. It wasn't like I didn't already believe her.

When we had our backs turned to Roy, Delilah also handed me a bottle of pills separate from the others. The label said Haldol. "For terminal states of delirium," she said. I didn't even have the heart to ask how I'd know.

I showed Delilah to the door, which she opened herself, then walked through carefully. Like a nervous teenage boy, I blurted, "Can I call you again?"

She paused there on the front steps (I thought to consider), then murmured almost inaudibly, "He'll need diapers."

So I bought some. A few days later was the first time he needed my help with it. Wishing to ease the tension in the air while I wiped his ass, he decided to tell a joke: "Now you'll have plenty of practice for when you knock up some unfortunate young woman." I laughed, but only because I thought I owed him the satisfaction. I humored him. The smell clung to my hands even after the bundle fell to the bottom of the garbage bin outside. From then on we knew better than to speak before it was done.

In Stevie's room the medical personnel weren't individual persons. It was more like a presence, a fully-conscious composite of faces and name tags and stethoscopes purposed with comforting loved ones. It spoke constantly, confidently. It never left the room.

Delilah left two weeks ago.

.

It's easy to believe ourselves stronger than we really are, so long as we're allowed to linger in the peripheral of life's suffering, at its safer edges. Before I met Roy, I would've flatly denied that any circumstances justified a person in taking their own life, or in asking someone else to take it for them. Now I think that we're all susceptible to these questions, given the right conditions, the right variety of trauma. My mother, for instance, seemed to ask with every depressed mannerism she developed whether life was worth living. Those questions never posed themselves to Stevie. He arrived at the hospital unresponsive and never came out of it. He didn't dwell consciously in that narrow space between here and after to really suffer. Neither did Roy's wife, from what I understand. Some might call this luck.

When we met in that bar by the freeway, Roy said that he didn't have the heart to put a bullet in his head. Too much pride, he said. We never spoke about it, but I guess maybe that's why I'm here. We never spoke about it.

Two days ago, Roy asked someone for a drink. I didn't know who, though I was the only one in the room. He'd been uneasily sliding in and out of himself all afternoon, making me nervous. For whatever reasons, he refused to take the Haldol. Probably because he sensed that it would be more for my benefit, for my immediate comfort, than his own. Some actions admit things we could never voice, things we'll never be ready to give up. I asked what he wanted, since I hadn't seen any alcohol in the house. His eyes widened for a moment, darting to different corners of the porch.

Finally his gaze settled on a spot inches below my chin. He deeply inhaled a breath, then coughed mucus that landed on my chest.

"In the pantry," he said. "Behind a sack of flour."

A dying man's wish. Just to help him sleep, he assured me. How could I deny him? To my surprise, there actually was a bottle tucked in the back of the pantry, an unopened pint of cheap vodka. Out of a slippery and indefinable sense of duty, of obligation, I carried the liquor back into the porch and set it on the nightstand beside Roy's bed. He stared through the window at his yard in the sunset. The trees surrounding the home fractured the sun's dimming light, cutting the overgrown grass in front of the windows into uneven blades of fuzzy color. It had been storming all afternoon, but cleared up an hour before. I couldn't tell exactly what he saw.

"Roy."

He heard me but not me. Without turning from the window, his voice coming from another world, teetering on an edge, he said, "It sure is dark in here, son."

He was right. The lights inside were turned off. I stepped across the wood floor to the switch by the doorway, flipped it on. One of Roy's hands shook wildly in the air, groping for the alcohol. The fingers unsuccessfully worked the cap, nearly knocking the plastic bottle off the table. I moved closer. His other hand clenched itself into a fist, curling at the wrist.

I firmly grasped the groping hand, and asked, "Can I help you?"

Squinting in the brightness, he moved his head up and down, sobbing now.

I reached over the bed, opening the bottle and lifting it to his lips. He gulped uncertainly at first, sputtering from the burn, then kept drinking. Clear liquid spilled from the pink corners of his mouth. When I pulled the bottle away, a third of it was gone. He gasped for air.

Once the liquor took effect, he calmed down some. His hands rested limp at his sides and his face dissolved into a puddle.

He said, "I wasn't sure if I wanted you here, but I'm glad you came."

"Who?"

"Your sister would've cried too much. Just like your mother."

I didn't want to lie, play the part of his son, so I fed him the bottle again. Fifteen minutes later it was gone. Roy's eyelids fluttered and his breath came in short bursts, his body seemingly restarting itself. I started to worry, to regret. Noises escaped from his throat, bubbling and gagging, but nothing came up. He started sobbing again, then weeping. A confused fit of anxiety and fear possessed him, piercing through his inebriation. Utterly lost in a life he couldn't recognize, in his dim and empty house, he screamed, "I can't see anything! I can't see anything!"

"It's okay," I said. "There's nothing left to see."

He stopped squirming and writhing, and I could've sworn he knew my voice for an instant. The look in his eyes was as good as a request.

I rolled him on his side, and pressed three of the fentanyl patches along his ridged spine. He didn't say anything else when I rolled him back over. Soon he was asleep. I watched for an hour, wondering if this is all it is, if being alive is merely being able to die.

But then he didn't die. He still hasn't, I just checked. I look out the windows. I study the pictures. I choose not to respond to the text my father sends, the one where he says he's filing for divorce. I open the door to the kitchen pantry, which happens to be about the size of a janitor's closet, and shut myself inside. That's when I realize the landline has been plugged in since I called the nurse. I never heard it before, but it's ringing now.

Sarah Evans

Only Human

I stop by the ward to look in on my patient. Miniature fingers fist tight and then unfurl, like a time-lapse flower. Her tiny mouth stretches in a yawn and within her pink baby-grow her legs curl up into her body as she mewls, lacking the strength for a full-throttled cry. Then the baby opens her eyes – ocean-deep blue – her gaze appearing so fully human.

Amidst the oxygen tubes and drips, she looks peaceful. The muscle degeneration and neurological impairment is not immediately apparent, nor the fact that future development can only go one way. Observing Lucy does not provide proper information; the scans and tests do that. I want to try and see what her parents see. The parents whom I am scheduled to meet in my office right now.

I swivel on squeaking rubber heels, conscious of the need for speed. I follow the well-worn route, corridors and stairs, glimpsing trees tipping into autumn gold beyond the windows. I spot the couple before they see me, two figures sitting hunched on plastic chairs, leaning into one another for support, hands clasped in a dual fist.

'Emily and Ryan,' I say. 'Thank you so much for waiting. We're just in here.' I blend brisk efficiency with a sympathy smile. What I have to say is hard and there is no point pretending that soft-soap lead-ins will lessen the hurt.

I seat myself behind my desk and name plate – *Amanda Richmond* – and indicate the seats on the other side. I put my glasses on and bring images up on my screen, peering intently as if gathering my thoughts, though I already know what I must say.

I keep my reading lenses on, maintaining the couple at an unfocussed distance. 'So we now have the results of the latest brain scan,' I say. I try to hold blurry eye contact, but they're determined to look anywhere but at me. 'I'm afraid the scan confirms what we've talked about.' All the medical indications are that Lucy lacks the capacity for any kind of conscious thought or meaningful awareness. Her brain damage is catastrophic and irreversible. Her movements and so on are pure reflex, a function of the more primitive brain stem which remains lesserly impaired. She is kept alive only via the intensive support we provide.

The way ahead is painful, but straightforward. Surely this couple will see that.

Nothing seems to register on their faces. Emily nudges Ryan. He coughs. 'We've been doing our own research online.' Inwardly, I groan at the words which every doctor dreads. 'We're not convinced everything's been tried yet.'

He starts talking about some doctor from Eastern Europe, whom they have contacted via social media. Ask any question on Google and someone will give you the answer that you want. I have had to get used to this over the years, parents deceiving themselves that their own unqualified research counts for more than my decades of training and medical practice. Ryan churns out technical terms, their complexity proving there must be something to it.

'These aren't orthodox methods,' I say. I point out that this so-called doctor has not examined Lucy, nor seen her files. It is so very clear that he is peddling pseudoscience, infecting anguished minds with false hope. I continue on, emphasising the full extent of damage and the expertise within this hospital, all the while sensing my grip on the situation slithering away. Why believe the person offering professional truth, when another offers what you long to hear?

Emily starts talking now, describing how the child

responds to a mother's touch, how she enjoys being kissed and tickled and cuddled. 'I know that she's in there.' Clinical knowledge cannot compete with knowledge born of love. Alien images on a screen do not impinge on what she thinks she sees, her observance filtered by the lens of desperation.

I swallow back all I'd like to say. *Keep it simple.* 'It may seem like that. I know how hard this is.' Certainly I have been here many times, though only from my side of the table.

We reach a pause. I breathe in, the scent of disinfectant and sweat. 'We need to discuss next steps,' I say.

The two of them snap to hyper-alertness. 'Meaning?' Ryan's tone turns instantly hostile.

It's the part of my job I hate. The flipside of offering people hope, of providing treatment and sometimes cures, is that the story doesn't always end that way. 'We need to consider options.' We are out of options.

'Options?' Ryan echoes back, perched on his cliff-edge of anger.

I talk about how Lucy may be suffering, pain not registering on her face or in her cries, because she lacks the power for those outward manifestations. How she has no future. I lead into the only possible solution. 'We need to think about removing life support.' This is as soft and evasive as I can manage. This baby must be allowed to gently die. I have no doubts that this is for the best.

'You can't do that.' Ryan's face turns red and his fist descends onto the desk separating us. Weariness takes hold. Hostility feels an unfair response to my hardworking efforts.

Emily's features crumple into anguish and she sinks

her head down into her hands.

I need to remain in control. Need to defuse things. 'Nothing needs to be decided today.' Untrue. The decision is all but made. But for now it's enough to put the idea out there – as if it hasn't been there ever since Lucy developed symptoms of this rare and untreatable degenerative condition – in the hope that gradually it will sink in. I suggest that we schedule a meeting with the full medical team once the two of them have had time to think things over.

Emily's eyes snap up to look into mine. 'We'll take her out of here if we have to,' she says. 'You can't stop us.'

I hold her gaze. *Please may it not come to this.* 'We'd have to follow the proper discharge process,' I say. 'We'll talk again.'

They stand abruptly and leave. The appointment has overrun, meaning other fraught parents have been left waiting. I feel empty. But there are other babies who have a real chance and I owe them and their families my very best by way of energy and attention.

I brace myself to carry on with my day.

The morning of the meeting, I wake to the dawn chatter of birds and an underlying disquiet. I chew on muesli and switch on the TV, discovering that the Newman baby has made breakfast news. Emily and Ryan sit on a plush sofa in matching pink T-shirts printed with the slogan: *Save baby Lucy.* They present their heartbreak, highly selective with the facts, and appeal for funds to pay for pioneering treatment abroad. A photo goes up of the baby at her most beatific, the tubes and so on tucked away.

I switch the TV off.

Arriving at work, I have the usual pressing things

to do, reading through requests for new referrals, checking test results. But this can't wait. I bring up Lucy's notes onscreen and I think about the training courses I have been on and the procedures that I hoped never to have to use. *If the parents raise the money and want Lucy discharged, could we let her go?* The decision is not mine to take, not singly, but I am at the centre. It is best to flag potential problems early. I compose an email, copying in all relevant personnel: other medical staff involved in Lucy's care, a senior manager, the Named Nurse for Safeguarding Children, the in-house legal team. I word things neutrally, running through the medical facts and referring to the TV interview. I suggest we meet to consider our position in case the usual route for persuasion fails. I deal in life, yet every argument, every instinct tells me that the best outcome for this child is that she die and without delay. This is my job and it's my patient I am answerable to, not her parents.

I reread and press send.

My day goes from bad to worse, my time poorly spent as constantly I'm sidetracked from my usual programme of care to deal with the flurry of responses and questions. The meeting with Lucy's parents does not go as hoped. Ryan and Emily stare down at the floor as I repeat my views. They have brought along a lawyer and leave him to do the talking, reeling out his stock phrases, constantly reiterating the legal assumption of a parent's right to make decisions about their own child.

These are loving parents; they want the best for their baby.

But love sometimes leads people astray.

Days accumulate. First frost nips at the air. The press

latch on and the fund-raising campaign goes viral. Lucy keeps on breathing with the help of the machine. She gains a little weight with the aid of the intravenous drip. Her muscles weaken, but she can still manage lacklustre movement, kicking her legs, fisting and releasing fingers. None of this means much. None of it indicates what is – or rather is not – going on inside her brain.

The East European doctor is pictured in the papers, broad-chested and with a puffed-up air. He has new therapies which are proven to work even in no-hope cases, so he claims, his smile smug. Clearly he is loving every moment of free marketing and I'm sure it is doing his quack practice the world of financial good.

I spend an evening researching him, sitting bent over my laptop with a growing headache. Could he could be right, a wonder cure popping up right on cue? It isn't as if I wouldn't be delighted if it did. But I have never believed in miracles and his regime of herbal supplements and physical therapy sounds vastly inadequate to combat this complex condition with its ramifications for every area of neural development. I read thoroughly. Cynically.

From the little I can find, I deduce that his sample size is tiny. The children he has treated are nowhere near as sick as Lucy. He has not followed proper clinical procedure with a double-blind control group, making his self-reported results no more than anecdotal and, as any scientist knows, anecdotal evidence is no evidence at all.

I read and read and convince myself of what I already know: this man comes with the name *charlatan* written right through.

Trying to relax with a glass of wine, I ponder what he hopes to gain when his attempts at treatment fail. No doubt the blame will be placed on us, on me, for any delay in moving Lucy. The positive publicity of having tried will outweigh the negative publicity of having failed and what kind of crazy logic is that?

Wind blows leaves across my windscreen as I drive to work. I am sharp with the junior doctor who does not pick up on things as quickly as he ought to, impatient with everyone as constantly I am taken away from my real work, forced to respond to requests from our legal and press teams, judging how best to answer journalists and phrase public statements, making sure not to prejudice our legal position. Confrontation in court seems increasingly inevitable and we seek Queen's Counsel advice, needing to ensure that we win. *Win* does not seem the appropriate term.

I rearrange one of my clinics, patients left waiting longer than they ought to, and a group of us head to Lincoln Fields. The quiet squares with their old buildings set around central greens take me back to college days. *Doctor or lawyer*: those were the options proposed for a bright ambitious girl. *Lawyer* sounded dull. *Doctor* sounded uplifting, doing good, saving lives.

Here I am arguing over death.

The office is shabbier than I expect, surfaces piled high with papers, bulging bookshelves lining the walls, reminding me of an Oxford tutor's room; the air is chilly after the warmth of the wards. The QC is younger than I imagined, more sceptical, when I anticipated her being easily convinced and fully on our side. She *is* on our side, of course, on the side of whoever pays her. She needs to delve deep into all the awkward questions, testing the robustness of our case, so that she can best prepare and advise us. I understand these things, even as I feel resentment rise; this is my area of professional expertise and I am used to being trusted in my judgement.

I do not doubt my own truths, but medicine is not physics and there are no absolute laws. Diagnosis, prognosis: these are based on clinical opinion, on finely tuned reason derived from long years of study and accrued experience.

I cannot say with certainty how much the baby suffers.

I cannot know how it feels to be her, what her body and mind experience.

I cannot say how long she might live on life support before even that fails.

I cannot prove that this other doctor is wrong, not other than by letting him have a go, by waiting and observing. *See! Told you so!* That is not an option we can contemplate.

The legal threshold for overruling the parents and detaining Lucy, for removing life-support without their consent, is rightly high. The easier course is to discharge her. It would make Emily and Ryan happy, albeit briefly, would make my life simpler and allow resources to be directed to other patients in need. Does it matter if the baby silently suffers? It's no more than the suffering of an animal and we inflict plenty of that.

But this is not the way I have ever thought. For all that Lucy has less than a normal baby's awareness, she is still fully human. I cannot sign off discharge papers without abandoning my duty of care. The baby's interests are at the heart of my job and I cannot walk away.

Autumn sun dapples through leaves onto my desk. My in-tray is piled high with day-to-day important business and I make my way steadily through. I reach for an envelope addressed to *the doctor treating baby Lucy*. I hesitate, before opening it. Light dances across the page; the word *Murderer* screams at me in capital letters. I sit for a moment to allow my pulse to settle. Carefully I screen out anything not properly addressed to me by name and I place these in an internal envelope, mark it for the legal team's attention, and put it in my out-tray.

I try to control the inner shaking as I get on with my day.

This is just the start. In meetings, the press office updates the team on what is going on. Letters arrive in increasing numbers with their abusive language and death threats, and there's an irony in the latter which provokes the bitterest of smiles. The twitter feed is bombarded, people replying to our hope-filled messages with the language of hate. The switchboard is swamped with obnoxious calls. Newspaper headlines pander to the emotional circus and ignore the facts.

Everyone feels entitled to their uninformed opinions: on Lucy, on the hospital, on me and my team.

Late in the evening, I visit the baby. I try to place myself in her mother's footsteps, to understand the depth of instinctive love she feels. *Our tiny Amazon princess*: that is the phrase Emily uses in the media, the innate clinging to life of a damaged body turned into a feisty fight. I have no children myself. Does this leave me ill-equipped for this case, or better equipped? If I had ever chosen to become pregnant, I would have gone for every available scan and most likely terminated a severely disabled foetus. In certain carefully prescribed circumstances, I would like the option of my own assisted suicide. In neither these cases can I determine my actions outside of the situation itself. *How would it actually feel?* At what point does scientific reasoning not provide the answer? Can the breath of life be precious in itself, set against the alternative of nothingness?

These questions have no answers and exhaustion bites as I make my way across the car-park, the day already slipped into darkness. They're upon me before I properly realise what is happening, a group of people brandishing placards surround me, blocking my way, faces distorted and inhuman with anger, voices chanting something I cannot catch. One of them spits, the gob landing on my sleeve. I push forward, fumbling for my car keys. I drive blindly away then pull into a side street and sit there, knuckles glowing white under a full moon as I grip the steering wheel, waiting for my hands to steady.

I breathe slowly in, slowly out, filling my lungs with air-freshener and fake leather.

Murderer. The red painted word keeps flashing before my eyes. I ponder the distillation of emotion to this pure and primitive form, the passionate conviction in being right despite not having any of the facts, the delusion these people are under that they are caring individuals, caring about a child they do not know and fervently believing that their so-called *caring* gives them the right to cause stress and harm to others.

I believe that I am right too. That's not the same.

End of week and I feel drained, much more than usual. I head for a college reunion, meeting up with friends I haven't seen for years. It's my chance to get away from it all, an opportunity to relax and enjoy nostalgia conversation and good food and wine.

Two decades ago and we were the closest of friends. With passing time, contact has fallen away, not helped by my long hours and weekends on call, and of course the others have busy lives too.

I dress up far more glam than usual and stare at

myself in the mirror, trying to conjure that teenage girl starting out here so full of idealism, endlessly memorising complex Latin terms and learning not to faint during human dissections, looking ahead to a career of helping people. Over a formal dinner, a different wine with every course, everyone seems less worn than me; they seem more content. I provide the upbeat version of my life, the stylish flat overlooking the Thames, the satisfaction from my work, the travelling to conferences and exotic holidays. My narrative emerges flat. It does not compete with the accounts of family life, as others mock-complain about the difficulties of raising kids – *it never gets any easier* – as if I've had a lucky escape. I think how it was never my intention that work become my primary focus to the exclusion of other possibilities, yet somehow things have fallen out that way.

We're onto the cheese and port before the inevitable happens: someone links up the name of the hospital I work at with the newspaper headlines. *Isn't that where...?* I admit, that yes, I know about the case, yes, I'm involved, yes, these cases are difficult. I can't really discuss it. For legal reasons and to protect patient confidentiality.

These are intelligent, educated people and they see my side to things, offering downward smiles. *It must be a nightmare.* I smile tightly, not wanting to dwell on my current preoccupations, this fight for something I believe, fighting so that a child can be allowed to die. Not the kind of battle I ever anticipated.

The conversation moves on. My talk remains bright, my laughter forced. I drink more than I ought to and it does not help me to unwind. I excuse myself early and retreat to a room in the grandly ancient quad and wonder whether the rooms were always this dingy, the beds so narrow, the air so unheated and scented with mildew. I lie awake until the early hours, listening to the noise of people stomping the corridors, to their rapid talk and high-pitched mirth, the sounds of other people having a good time.

The clocks change, mornings becoming lighter, evenings darker. The protests escalate. Campaigners gather every day, sometimes a dedicated two or three whose faces I come to recognise, other times a bigger group. Each morning and evening I am confronted by slogans borrowed from pro-life campaigns. *Every life matters. Don't let me die. Murderers.* I try to find compassion for empty lives, people living off borrowed sentiment and imagining what they feel is real. I try and fail.

The protesters harass everyone and anyone who enters and exits the building. Doctors, nurses, auxiliary staff. They do not spare the agitated parents of other very sick children.

What makes them think they have the right?

The boiling up of fury does nothing to help me ease into my working day.

But public opinion works both ways and I hear that Emily and Ryan are receiving abuse too. Some tiny *only-human* part of me feels the beat of satisfaction; the much larger part is appalled. I have spent decades studying the brain. Its workings seem ever more incomprehensible.

I meet with the head of HR who pours me strong coffee and asks how I am bearing up. 'We're here to support you,' she says. I present her with my capable, coping face. 'I'm impressed at how well you're dealing with this,' she says. I'm simultaneously relieved and disappointed at her failure to see though my thin veneer.

Increasingly, I am not coping. I sleep badly. I wake too early, unrefreshed and I startle at every unexplained noise. I dread my arrival at work and once inside I struggle to achieve the mental concentration required to focus on my other patients, the children I can use my skills to actually help. I no longer take a brisk, head clearing walk during my lunch break. I avoid the radio, TV, papers and internet, cutting myself off from the world. Until a periodic and perverse curiosity takes hold and I binge online, discovering things I later regret knowing.

And all the while, the unknowing centre of all this animosity remains part of my ward round. The basics are written up on Lucy's chart, the daily checks of weight, pulse, reflex and blood tests. She sleeps longer and moves less.

I schedule another scan and the results are worse than expected. This helps our case, and rapid decline seems kinder than the alternative, but I do not feel glad. I feel the recurring sadness for this tiny scrap of an unformed being, her potential never to be realised, an unlucky quirk of genetics determining her fate.

The court case is scheduled urgently; I reschedule appointments so that I can spend my day in court. English law is based on an adversarial approach, even here when the issue is a sick child. Our lawyer versus that of the parents.

My breath mists in the frozen air as my smart shoes clack their way to the grandiose entrance of the building which houses the family court. Protesters have gathered in their many dozens, brandishing banners and chanting their songs and I keep my eyes down, refusing to read the placards or to look into eyes which likely glow with self-righteousness. I wonder what they think they will achieve, whose mind or heart they hope to influence by being here; surely the law is objective. These are not the right questions. These people are taking action to save the life of an innocent child; I am the heartless bitch with her death sentence.

The point of today's proceedings is for someone learned and impartial to hear both sides of the argument and deliver a judgement on a legal question. I have nothing to fear from external scrutiny. If the hospital is overridden on a point of law, that does not undermine my medical opinion. Yet sitting in the cold impersonal room, waiting for things to begin, I feel gut-tight with nerves, as if I am on trial.

Slowly things get underway, formal niceties and opening remarks are made. The wooden benches are uncomfortable as I sit and listen to Emily. She is visibly agitated, inarticulate with heartache, not particularly well educated. Might the judge be moved? But like doctors, it is not a judge's job to respond to naked emotion.

Tension ratchets up as the moment for my testimony approaches. Taking my place in the witness box, delivering my secular oath, looking out at the people crowding the small room, I feel an upswell of panic which has no rational basis. My vision blurs and my mind blanks. *I can't do this.* But as our lawyer starts with her lead-in questions and my time to speak comes, nerves fall away, the way they have done in so very many exams. Outwardly I am calm and persuasive. Even when the questioning flips to the parents' lawyer, becoming harsher, the inner tremble does not show. I slip into my performance, the words I need appearing on demand, the more hostile the probing, the more incisive my responses; I know my stuff, have only to let it flow with unruffled certainty. Emily may have appealed to sentiment, but surely rational argument takes its natural place in a court of law.

I want to win. I want to be proved right. But only because I firmly believe that I am.

Days pass, the weather is grey and wet, and constantly I feel the underlying strain of waiting; another mind is deciding something which has become so personal to me. I replay everything that I did and did not say from the stand and wonder if I could have expressed things more persuasively. I try to look ahead. This will be over soon, one way or the other, and I can return to a life where my preoccupation is patient care, free from the distractions and the daily upset of all that hate.

Please may the judge rule in our favour.

He does; victory does not feel sweet.

And of course nothing is over yet. Mentally, I plead with the parents not to appeal. *Just accept things.* Unsurprisingly, this has no effect. I watch Ryan's earnest face on TV as he explains their decision to carry on fighting. How can someone be so sure, so well-meaning, and yet so misguided?

The process goes on and on, everything fast tracked yet it seems to take some kind of forever. The baby's vital signs continue to decline. The protestors increase in number and aggression. The hospital loses valuable members of staff to jobs elsewhere and absenteeism is high. Parents turn up to appointments even more distraught than usual. The newspaper headlines and the news items never end.

I feel pushed to my human limits. I make an error in prescribing and though it is picked up by the nurse, no harm done, it leaves me shaken. I worry about decisions, dither over diagnoses, order more tests than necessary, schedule unneeded follow ups, my limited time squeezed ever tighter until it feels like I am going to explode. I consider changing career, something with defined office hours and far removed from life and death. Alternatives are much harder to imagine than first appears. Here I am with all those A-star GCSEs and A levels, my university degree from Oxford and all the many hurdles of my training. What do I know how to do which isn't this? What do I know of business, or economics, or management?

Each appeal drives me further under; the parents look close to drowning too as each appeal fails. Finally, the avenues for higher opinions run out and the hospital is free to move the baby to hospice care for her final days. I see Lucy one last time before she leaves, this baby who has formed the centre of so much heightened feeling; she lies entirely still, too weak to move, yet to an untrained eye she could simply be sleeping.

I feel sorrow for a life which never really started, the journey cradle to grave far too short. I feel sorrow for the grief of Emily and Ryan. But all the acrimony lingers like slow-acting poison in my blood. Returning to my office, I wait for the relief which does not arrive.

I take leave for Christmas, family time with my sister, nieces and mother, plus a few days away in the sun. I'll feel better for the break. I tidy up my office and send numerous emails in preparation for my absence. One of the legal team appears at my door.

'It's over,' he says. 'An hour ago.'

I nod. It's the right outcome, but it hardly makes me happy.

'I've something for you,' he adds, and hands across a stack of opened envelopes. A junior employee has been given the task of sifting through my post, making sure I receive all clinical correspondence, whilst protecting me from the hate-mail. Personal letters which have nothing to do with baby Lucy have been wrongly held back.

I take a card out of the largest envelope, revealing a roughly drawn fir tree strewn liberally with glitter that will get everywhere, remnants of it re-emerging over the coming months. Inside, two handwritten messages appear alongside a photo. Adult writing says, *We will always remember what you did for us.* Childish letters spell out *love Chloe.* The picture shows a bright-eyed girl, shining with life, and I remember back to a very sick baby. I sit and stare at the image awhile before working my way through the other cards and messages. *This is why,* I remind myself. Then I gather my things and head out to the empty car-park, the air cold and clear, a sprinkling of snowflakes falling softly on my face and stars glinting in the void above.

Jeff Ewing

Fireball Outfit

"Everywhere you look's a circus." That's how our Uncle Whelp put it, preaching from the third floor balcony of our grandparents' house, a house situated within a shrinking semi-wilderness he'd left just once at the age of seventeen, and had returned to drawn forever inward, done, a "fireball outfit" in the terminology of the big top he'd adopted. People around town called him other things; I won't bother to repeat them. I've had similar names used against me and would just as soon leave them back there. As kids, we of course sided with Uncle Whelp. The last thing we wanted to be around was another successful adult on his run-of-the-mill way. Eccentricity was a godsend, like a snow day or a passing mid-week fever.

Sun fell on the wide lawn after breaking through the branches of the pine to spotlight him there above us, calling out his cryptic commands: "Cheops dazzle," or "Flay the whiskered darling," or "Alight the corbel." We'd do what we thought he wanted—form ourselves into human pyramids, spin in dizzying arm-splayed circles, tumble in unison through clouds of dandelion spores. Obedient and content we flung ourselves in this way down the long slope of August, up to the morning when, in executing a near-perfect "lace the parcel," my sister Claire overshot to thump against the plank wall of the tool shed. Her eye pressed to a gap between boards a moment later, she released a startled squeak. I pushed her aside and saw for myself the outline of the wheeled sled resolve slowly from the haze of dust.

Sidney and June joined us, stumbling down the lawn, barking in quick yips: "me first me first me first". Claire and I hauled the door open, disturbing the long-established equilibrium of the shed's interior, altering its internal weather to such an extent that within a matter of months it would be unrecognizable—snow drifted into the corners, the yard tools frozen and abandoned. Behind us, Uncle Whelp hollered further commands, unaware that we were elsewhere. The sled's wheels were patinaed with rust, big flakes layered like scales.

"It's gonna need oil," I said.

Sidney found some on a high shelf, thick and dark as syrup. After several dousings the wheels began to move and soon were spinning freely. We oiled the pivot of the handle too, freeing up the steering mechanism. June rubbed the wood body with a rag. Slowly the name Flexi Flyer appeared like revealed code, then the picture of a child's face distorted by joy, screaming with it, the wind of descent raking a cresting wave of hair back in near freefall. Below this irresistible illustration were my father's initials, etched into the wood in an immature scrawl. Of course, it couldn't really have been him— with his scowl and his chin thrust in disappointment at our every misstep. He had never felt that wind, I was sure, or screamed from ignorance and thrill the way the kid in the picture was doing, and we soon would.

"Back to show, my children," Uncle Whelp called out. It was always just "show", he'd insisted on that numerous times. Never "the show". A circus moved at such speeds that no common article could hope to keep up.

"Show is everything," he emphasized.

We ignored him, fully possessed now by the sled and its promise. It was the first time I could recall us disobeying one of his injunctions. Our visits had always been lightly altered repetitions of previous visits; meals and recriminations, the four of us kids diving into the wilderness of the house and the yard that was gradually making its way back into woods. But my grandmother's death had knocked things off track and taken some final softness out of the place. My parents' raised voices rang louder, and Uncle Whelp's animation came across as desperate and forced.

He leaned far out and called again: "Tent!"

Again we ignored him, and I felt the ground go unsteady under me with our rebellion, a tremor he may have felt likewise shudder through the balcony rail. His presence there above us had always been reassuring, and vaguely threatening, as god or Jesus or Moses must have been to those friends of mine who went to church and believed in intangible things. I'd been only once myself, for the funeral of the father of a kid in my class who'd been decapitated by a falling boulder up in the mountains. Thankfully, there was no headless body to greet us, as I'd been afraid there might be, just a long, polished coffin with what there was left of his father inside. Discontinuous and rotting, as I pictured him, waiting his chance to reassemble and chastise his son. As I imagined my father would have done in comparable circumstances.

Or maybe he would have just laid there, relieved. At the moment he was inside and fully intact, sorting through our grandparents' things. The effort made him more irascible than usual. There was just too much stuff—the rooms were swollen with it—and Uncle Whelp wasn't helping. We had hoped there might be less fighting under the circumstances, but Uncle Whelp could get under my father's skin faster than anyone.

"He's never accommodated himself to life," was how my mother put it.

"Bullshit," my father said.

Whenever the subject of Uncle Whelp's stagnation—his "redo childhood" as my grandmother once called it—came up, my father would tuck his head down into his neck and cross his arms tight across his chest. He saw it as an unfair trade, I think, suspecting the only way my uncle could have that childhood was by him giving his up.

"He just doesn't want the headache of being an adult," he said. Something I hadn't realized until then was even an option, like setting or not setting the table.

I sat on the grass with the others, my back itchy where my shirt had ridden up. I heard a flock of geese pass overhead and looked up to watch the near-perfect vee move north, marred by an errant goose at the end of one arm lagging behind and then flapping madly to catch up again. It looked ridiculous, and familiar.

#

The story we heard was that Uncle Whelp had followed a girl west, then lost her somewhere outside Kansas City.

"Heartbroken," my mother said.

"Everything heals," my father countered.

Wishful thinking in Uncle Whelp's case, who sat in his car at the edge of a cow pasture the morning after the nominative love of his life had left him, watching a bank of fog coalesce around him. A miasma materializing in his reckoning directly from his heartbreak, the outgassing of a condition as real as polio or the flu. Moving outward from his vena cava to smother the pastureland for miles, clear to the banks of the Mississippi, from which direction clowns and animal handlers now emerged to pass on either side of him, vaporous in the dew that soaked his jean cuffs as he followed them to the variegated tent laid out, the elephants—as he'd always imagined—hoisting the poles into place. Massive timbers knotted with fist-sized whorls. Someone handed him a rope, and—as he told it to us—with that adopted him into a new family, one without grudges, expectations, or judgment. I was just a kid at the time, but even I knew better.

I asked my dad once why he hated Uncle Whelp so much. The question surprised him, I think.

"I don't," he said. "I don't know what you'd call it, but it isn't hate."

A box of oranges sat open on the kitchen table, sent all the way from Florida by an army buddy of my grandfather's. The label caught my eye, beautiful and absurdly elaborate—a panther mid-leap, one paw out and teeth bared. What panthers had to do with oranges I couldn't imagine, but I guessed that wasn't the point. My dad took out three of the oranges and, as if this were how he started every morning, began to juggle them. It was impressive, if rudimentary at first; then he began building, adding more oranges to the effortless ellipse, one after another until a nearly unbroken ring of subdued fire spun between us. It was mesmerizing. He kept them going for an impossible length of time and didn't drop a single one; not a bruise was imparted. Then he shuttled them in a graceful arc back into the box and replaced the lid.

"Anyone can do it," he said.

#

Claire took the first run, which was only fair. She'd spotted the sled and seen its worth through the accumulation of rust and neglect. Uncle Whelp had come out the back door, but he wouldn't go farther than the steps. He looked at the gravel drive and the road beyond as if it were a river raging by.

"They tried to shoot the human cannonball across the Mississippi once," he said. "The sky there you wouldn't believe, stretched so tight you could hear the wind bumping against it. The guy bounced right off, ended up somewhere down the river for fish food."

There was never much traffic on the road where it swept up over the hill and past the drive. June and Sidney held Claire's feet on the gravel shoulder.

"You ready?"

"Almost."

I took a slow step toward them, my mouth just opening to yell, late as always.

"That's a yes to me," Sidney said, falling backward.

Outside the back door, just visible through the wall of bushes, Uncle Whelp had produced his accordion and was playing a circus melody, droning and falsely optimistic. Our raised voices might have sounded like discordant singing to him at that distance, the doppler-ing whine of the approaching car's engine as it crested the hill and started down little more than an off note.

The wheels of the sled rattled downhill, throwing handfuls of gravel back at us. One chipped the lens of June's glasses, an imperfection she peered around for the next two years. Even after it was replaced, she claimed the blind spot persisted, the way a scratch on a record could become—in the days of records—part of the song.

Uncle Whelp's accordion warbled like a train whistle bearing down as the sled latched onto the ends of Claire's hair and Rapunzeled up to lodge tight against her scalp. The sudden tension yanked the steering bar hard left. We could see the driver and the woman beside him, maybe his wife, as they sped past, their eyes making the short journey from carefree to horrified with no stops in between. They veered sharply off the road and through the Jenkins' fence. There followed the thud of impact, and the crown of the big sycamore trembling over the road.

There was blood around the roots of Claire's tangled hair; a couple of dishwater tassels, torn free, waved from the wheel hub. We tried backing the sled out, unwinding the wheels, but it only tangled further. Claire swatted at us, kicking out with one foot. The other, we could see, was turned at an unnatural angle. The tip of a bone poked like a startled animal through her tanned skin.

June held the sled while Sidney and I carried Claire, walking as quickly and carefully as we could—with every bump or stumble came another rabbity shriek — back up the road and down the drive. When Uncle Whelp saw us, he stopped playing. The accordion fell lifeless against his chest, his hands flicking back and forth like lopped chicken heads. We had just come even with the wilted flower bed when he turned smartly on his heel and disappeared into the house, saying over his shoulder, "Tough luck, Bill." Our father's name, the last drawn-out consonant punctuated with the sharp click of the lock.

Sidney pounded on the door and hollered in a convincing replica of our father's voice: "Goddammit, Whelp, open this fucking door!" We didn't understand the ways people could come undone, and didn't at that moment care. It was our mother who finally appeared, and with a pair of poultry shears cut Claire free. She covered the break, the white of bone, with her hand, as if to save Claire some unspecified embarrassment. She ran her other hand along the jagged fringe of hair, beginning to cry and saying only now, "Oh no."

We left the Flexi Flyer where it fell. Everyone in the neighborhood gathered to watch the tow truck pull the car out of the Jenkins' little patch of woods and the ambulance take the man and woman away, their faces still registering the recent robbery of their surety. Claire got a cast out of it, and a short haircut all the way around. She never let it grow out again, keeping it short as a kind of anti-talisman. It would come in and out of style, but that never bothered her.

We took turns trying out her crutches, leaving punctures in the grass that formed little pools in the first rain a week later. Uncle Whelp appeared on the balcony and tried assembling us into his conscript circus, but we weren't having it. The coins he tossed down we let lie where they fell. After dinner he passed out handbills announcing a performance for that evening, a "show to end all shows". My dad crumpled the paper up and threw it away under the sink, into the black maw where generations of chicken livers and potato skins had been dispatched, along with the castoff rinds of half-forgotten slights and triumphs. A person might have learned something from the leavings, if they'd had the stomach for it.

The performance was a dud. Uncle Whelp entered without fanfare—a startling abdication of showmanship—then came to slow attention. He took the leaky old Hohner he'd won at euchre from the apocryphal, broken-toothed ring announcer out of its case and began to play "Knockout Drops". Just as he had on the last day of his new life, when he came to beaten and robbed by the people he'd thought of as his friends. Played and played until finally the police showed up and hauled him away from the ring of dead grass where the tent had stood, and where the audience had roared with each step of the horses, his enclosed universe infinitely bright with the night's uncertainty sealed off behind a gaudy, fraudulent tapestry.

When he was done, he stood there in his pressed suit and wept, big forlorn sobs, his face as pitiful and embarrassing as any jilted high school understudy.

I stood up and walked out; nobody stopped me. Behind me I heard my mother.

"That's enough, Whelp."

And it was. More than enough.

It must have felt like Kansas City all over again, the remembered river swelling in his mind out of the brush where Washington Lane crossed above the house—never mind that it was a warm, clear summer evening distinct from the morning when he woke battered and alone in the same fog that had with such clarity revealed the circus to him on that first glorious day. A fog he couldn't be sure wasn't of his own making, that seemed to pour out of him and that he spooned back in again in small mouthfuls, where it ate him from the inside out.

#

June piled pillows and blankets against the crack beneath the door to muffle the sounds of arguing.

"Poor Uncle Whelp," Claire said.

"Are you kidding?"

"It's not his fault."

"Maybe it's ours," Sidney said.

"No way," I said.

Though I knew it might have been, part of it anyway. We had, after all, dragged the sled out of whatever past it had been relegated to without due consideration of its history and ghosts.

June climbed up onto the bed and began pulling imaginary lines. At times like this, when our family seemed on the point of swamping, she liked to pretend the room—a cavernous, converted attic we stayed in when we visited—was a ship we'd commandeered. One by one the rest of us climbed up on the bed with her. Somewhere around midnight the rumble of voices began to subside beneath the high whistling sound that was our simulation of wind and waves. We drifted through the black night with no sign of land or hope of rescue, the sea stippled behind us with the remnants of fallen stars sizzling in our wake.

When Uncle Whelp left early the next morning, I watched him go from the dormer window set into the peak of the gable at the end of the room. I'm not sure why I decided to follow him. I'd like to think it was out of concern, but it was more likely just aimless curiosity. The sun was barely up, the sky not quite blue yet. I waved at my father as he drove past on his way to the train station, but he didn't see me, invisible among the wild dogwood and brambles. By the time I got to where his car was stopped he'd already pulled Uncle Whelp out of the creek and hauled him onto the bank. I watched from the bridge as he rolled him over and yelled the water out of him, watched it run down through the moss on the creek bank and back into the stream. I remember thinking that maybe it was the last of the fog spilling out of him, leaving him finally to burn up the rest of the way or collect himself for another try.

I didn't go down to join them, there didn't seem to be room. I waited where I was and listened for voices in the hiss of water passing under the bridge. When they finally climbed up the embankment onto the road they looked small, my father and his brother. Not much bigger than me. They talked for a little while; I think they'd forgotten about me, or maybe I didn't exist for them yet. I couldn't hear much of what they said, just my father—in a tone different from anything he ever used with us; softer, as if he might break something if he wasn't careful—saying, "You've got a better end in you than this."

They left the car where it was, half on the road and half off. My father picked up the worn-out accordion case and they headed back together toward the house. The case leaked a trickle of dirty water, snaking along the road behind them. Uncle Whelp took off his suit jacket and draped it over his shoulder. A little ways along my father sneezed twice, loudly, shaking the young leaves on the last of the elms. Farther west, out to Missouri and beyond, all the elms had died already. They wouldn't be back. My father sneezed again. His allergies were always bad at that time of year. Uncle Whelp held the sleeve of his jacket out, still dripping, as some pilgrim might on his way to Mecca or St. Louis. My father laughed and ran his nose obligingly down the length of it.

Dinner was peaceful that night, pork chops and apple sauce served on the china my grandparents had received as a wedding gift. Tiny horses were etched into the rims, for some reason, their tails looping back in delicate scrollwork. How intricate everything was once, I thought—or maybe that came later—how much thought went into the most inconsequential of creations.

David Frankel

Meadowlands

The tree tops are stirring against a milky sky. The hiss rises to a roar as the wind builds, rolling in waves through the highest boughs, but all that noise and motion are far above my head. Down here on the sodden ground the air is still and thick and I feel as though I am underwater.

Meadowlands is changing. The spruce are being replaced acre by acre, replanted with other trees. People dislike the conifers. They are foreign invaders. Their uniformity and the darkness beneath their closed ranks make them easy to hate, but I enjoy the silence they bring; the way their thick bed of needles and oily wood suck noise out of the air. They keep secrets. In the densest parts of the plantation you can't see more than a few meters. It's easy to lose your way in there, and people do; walkers coming down off the hills trying to take a shortcut. With no horizon to navigate by, they get confused by the false perspectives in the avenues between the trees. I hear them sometimes, crashing through the wood. Occasionally I find the prints of walking boots weaving through the plantation.

Out here, on the edge of the estate, the genteel parkland at its centre is a distant fantasy. You can scream all you want, nobody will come. I know this for a fact. When I first started working here, felling the spruce, I dropped a tree in the wrong direction and, before I could jump clear, it caught me across the ankle. I shouted for a long time before I realised just how alone I was. I limped back to the road where, at last, I caught a phone signal. Doyle came for me in the Land Rover. I had no one else to call.

'I've broken my ankle. It's fucked. Don't touch it.'

As usual, Doyle was unimpressed and reluctant to interrupt his cigarette. He made no attempt to touch it until we got back to the caravan we shared. He helped me in and dropped me on my bed. I picked at my laces while he rolled another cigarette. When he was ready, he said, 'I need to see it. Hold still.'

Holding his unlit cigarette between thin, pale lips he set about taking off my boot. I couldn't look. It hurt a lot, and finally he lost patience with my squirming and yanked the boot clear. Horror washed over his face.

'Jesus, lad. It's a fucking mess. They'll never be able to save that. I'm going for an ambulance. Your tree-felling days are over, son. Best you don't look.' He laid a tea towel gently across my foot so I wouldn't have to see the extent of my injuries. A spot of blood began to seep through the pattern. I tried to hold back tears as he dashed out of the caravan sobbing. It was only after he'd been outside for a while that I realised he was laughing.

'It's not funny. You fucking old bastard, Doyle.'

'Ah, you soft wee prick. It's a sprain. A couple of aspirin and a day sitting on your backside and you'll be fine. Here. Let me see. Can you move your toes? You're fine. I told you. Get a bag of peas on it.'

We didn't have any peas so I used a four-pack of lagers from the fridge.

Nobody but me comes out to the fringes of the plantation, not even the other estate workers. The owners probably don't even know these places exist. The trees have never been properly managed and they are cramped and raggedy. But, among the conifers are bright clearings where trees have fallen and sudden islands of life have sprung up in the middle of a dark green ocean. There is a network of overgrown tracks cut by forestry trucks decades ago, humid and humming with insects. They lead nowhere. Keep following them and they peter out. By the time you reach the deer-fencing at the edge of the moor, the paths have fanned out into sheep trails that climb through the heather to the steep slopes beyond the estate.

I prefer to work alone. That usually means following the main work party, clearing undergrowth and stacking logs. I love the smell of fresh cut timber and the fumes from the chainsaw mingling with the smell of my own body and the heavy, damp wool of my work jacket. But, every day can't be a winner: this week I'm working with Doyle. The underwater stillness of my secret clearings will have to wait.

I head back towards the middle of the estate. At this time of the morning, there will not be another soul on the miles of track that criss-cross the woodland. Later, the other men will be out working, and hill-walkers will arrive, but even around the loch, at the centre of the glen's wide belly, there are places nobody goes and the only sound is the water lapping quietly at its muddy banks.

I meet Doyle on the road. He's in the old Land Rover, driving up to meet me.

'How come you're up so early, young man? You shit the bed?'

'Just thought I'd go for a walk before work.'

'Glad you're feeling so energetic. Time to graft.'

I get in and he guns the engine. The failing drive-shaft clatters as the Landy labours its way along the steep, gravel track. It's a long, slow drive across the glen. We are repairing an access track beyond the loch. There are always road repairs to be done here. The erosion is constant. A slow peeling away of the surface by the streams that drain the uplands. The peat and forest stain the water dark red-brown as it gathers into broader arteries feeding the loch. The water is held back by an earth dam. The shallows around it are choked with silt and broad-leafed grasses, and the trees that grow along the banks are lank, reluctant, as though, instead of sustaining them, the water is drawing life from them.

The road skirts the loch closely, but the undergrowth is so dense, so entangled with the lower branches, that the water isn't visible. Still, I find myself staring into the darkness beneath the trees, unable to look away, straining for a glimpse. As we pass the end of the loch's access road I notice fresh tyre tracks. Someone must have been down to the water. A cold wave of nausea washes through my guts.

'See that! Someone's been down there.' I try to sound disinterested – only curious – but my voice is shaking.

'Aye. They're building a new drain.'

'A drain?'

'Aye. For the water levels.'

'When? Which part of the loch? When?'

'Soon. I don't know.' He looks at me, maybe suspicious, it's hard to tell with Doyle.

'When though? You must have heard something.'

'What the fuck does it matter? What's up with you? You been smoking your funny cigarettes again?'

I feel sick. If someone is poking around by the loch they'll find her, and when they do they'll ask around town and someone will tell them what happened at Killian's, and they'll come straight to me.

I'm still shaking when Doyle stops the truck and we start to unload our tools. As I'm throwing our picks and shovels onto the roadside, something on the track draws my attention: a tiny orb of gloss black. It is the eye of a young bird lying motionless between furrows of churned mud.

'Injured,' Doyle grunts.

I approach it slowly, cupping my hands around it. It barely moves until I lift it free of the mud. Injured though it is, I feel it pressing outwards against my palms, a warm fluttering, not just of its wings, but its whole body; a heartbeat, a tremble and an attempt at flight all joined in a single desperate rhythm. The tiny, black eye remains fixed on me as I place it on the turf bank beside the road and pile some leaves around it for protection.

Doyle is watching me with his piano-wire smile fixed. I feel myself blush. He thinks I'm soft, so I stand up and stamp on it, hard. Through the heavy sole of my boot the crunch is barely noticeable.

Doyle shakes his head, 'What the fuck did you do that for?'

'It'd die anyway.'

'If you say so, nurse.'

The physicality of digging calms me. I concentrate on the cutting of the ground with the spade and the weight of the wet earth as I lift it from the trench we're creating, but my mind is racing. If the girl wasn't naked they'd just think it was an accident, maybe.

Even after what happened in town there had to be other suspects in the frame. I tell Doyle about the townies who come to the car park on a Saturday night when the walkers have all gone home. 'They drive up here to smoke gear and fuck.'

One weekend, not long ago, I'd watched from a hiding place in the trees as two boys persuaded a girl to raise her skirt and show her arse. They gave her booze and got her to take her knickers off. I didn't want to see anymore so I threw the empty vodka bottle I'd been drinking from. It smashed against a tree and all three of them froze like animals, then ran for it, back to their car.

'There's no telling what would have happened if I hadn't been there,' I tell Doyle.

'What. The. Fuck. Are. You. On. A-bout?' He says each syllable slowly as though I'm a retard or something.

The caravan smells of butane and the dust burning on the bars of the electric fire. Doyle has the big bedroom, which we refer to as 'the master suite'. The second bedroom, just big enough for a bunk bed, stinks, so I sleep on the floor of the lounge area, using the sofa cushions for a mattress. At first I used to clear my makeshift bed away every morning, but not anymore. Occasional we get a temp worker staying here but neither of us likes having a guest and they never stay long. Not everyone can deal with Doyle.

After dinner, I drink too much. There is nothing else to do except listen to Doyle swearing at the portable TV while he exchanges texts with one of the other estate workers. Most nights, the other men take the Landy into town.

'Right, come on, laddy. Get your Old Spice on, we're away.'

'I'm not going.'

They'll only end up drinking at Killian's place again and after what happened last time, it's better I keep my head down. Besides, I'm tired from digging and anaesthetised by the beer.

'Suit yerself.'

He slams the door behind him and I hear his heavy booted feet trudging down the lane. I turn down the volume on the telly and open the windows. The beginnings of a headache are soothed by the damp gloom. I have a ciggie and listen to the soft hiss of rain on the ferns and grass that grow a meter high all around the 'van.

I smoke until the beer wears off, then sleep for a bit. When Doyle comes back from town he's brought me two and a half litres of Frosty Jack cider in a blue plastic bottle. He's always good like that, Doyle. The time I fucked up my ankle, he made me sandwiches so I wouldn't have to get off the bed, and he left me some beers and fags. He didn't even make me pay him back.

He's no angel though. He has a temper when he drinks. And he's been inside. He told me once, when he was pissed. I don't think he even remembers now that he told me. He said that was why he couldn't get a proper job and he was living in this dump with a dick like me. Obviously I asked what he did and how long he was in for, but he wouldn't tell me. Speaking into his nearly-empty beer can between gulps all he said was, 'I was in for long enough to find out you don't ask what people did. I paid my dues.'

I knew not to push Doyle, even when he was in a good mood, but I was feeling cocky, 'Were you guilty? Did you do it?'

'It doesn't matter. Once those bastards have got you in their sights, they don't care who they pin it on.'

That was all I got out of him.

When they find her, they'll check the records of everyone on the estate. Surely, they must. For the first time in days I feel a ray of hope. I take a long swig from the cider. 'Cheers, Doyle.'

For three days I dig nervously in the sun. On our day off it rains. Nobody fancies going to town. Not until later anyway. The humidity brings the midges out and the air in the caravan is choked with the smell of burning mosquito coils. The stinking smoke is probably poisoning us both but neither of us wants to be eaten alive.

If nobody is heading into town, there is nothing to do but drink and smoke. Whenever Doyle drinks there's the usual bullshit to deal with. One of the other grunts on the estate has been promoted — Pavel, a polish guy — and Doyle is fuming about it. I can't get the full story, and if I asked him it would make him worse.

'All these Poles and shite, takin' all the fuckin' jobs. I should be doin' that job. White niggers, that's what they are, I'm tellin' you.'

I figured out ages ago that when he's like this – pissed and worked up – it doesn't go well if you take him on. I grunt, as I usually do, and he takes it as a sign of agreement. In my mind I pretend I'd told him to fuck off. It's not like I give a shit, but he keeps on and on.

'For fuck's sake, Doyle. If you're so much better than him, how come he got the job.'

'Coz he's a fucking foreigner and we've all got to be politically bloody correct. And he's a fuckin' arse kisser.'

'Maybe you should pucker up, too.'

'What do you know? How old are you? You're fucking twelve or something. This your first job? Second? You know nothing.'

'Aye and bet I get a promotion before you do.'

'Don't you get smart with me you little bastard.'

'I can't stand this place. How come I've got to share this shit-box with you?'

'You can fuck off and sleep in the woods anytime you want to. You think I like having you under my fucking feet all the time.'

He is spitting angry. A piece of baked bean flies from his mouth and lands in his drink. It stops him, as though he's embarrassed or he's waiting to see if I've noticed. He stares at me for a moment, and I stare back, holding his gaze for a long time. Doyle can be pretty scary when he's like this, and I come close to shitting myself. When he jumps up I come even closer, but he just storms into his bedroom, still swearing to himself, and shuts the door. Through the flimsy wall I hear, 'You need a slap. Teach you some fucking manners.'

I get up and slam my plate down on the draining board. With a chipboard wall between us I feel braver. Standing in the caravan door with my hand on the latch, I shout, 'Fuck off you old bastard,' and duck out. As I stride up the track, the door is flung open and Doyle sticks his torso out. I get ready to run, in case he comes after me.

'Where the fuck are you going now?'

'Away from you and your racist gobshite.'

He slams the door.

I need to be on my own to think things through properly, calmly, without Doyle fucking with my head, so I head into the old plantation. Deep in the trees, so deep it's difficult to find even when you know it's there, is the ruin of a croft. The plantation must have grown up around it as its roof gave in to gravity and time. By the time I have fought my way through the undergrowth the sun is out. I stand in the humid air of the clearing for a moment, close my eyes and turn my face towards the sun. Around me are the sounds of birdsong and water dripping heavily from the trees.

The walls of the old house are broken by three

small windows and a narrow doorway. A hearth at one end of the only room is the only other feature. The grass covered floor is littered with stones from the slowly collapsing masonry. I turn one over to use its dry side as a seat and retrieve my tin from the chimney. Inside is a small, nearly empty bottle of whiskey, two porn mags and a couple of ready-made joints.

Soon, they'll search the woods. Men in fluorescent jackets walking through the trees in slow-moving lines. When they do, they'll find this place. They'll use it against me, insinuate things.

I light a joint and have a last, affectionate look through the magazines before pulling out the pages one at a time and making a fire of them. Staring, stoned, into the flames I watch disembodied limbs and genitals blacken and disappear.

I poke at the ash with a stick while I finish the whiskey. Looking around me, it's easy to believe the forest has been here forever, but Doyle reckons it was planted in the thirties. The people who lived in this little stone house could never have guessed that one day it would be lost under trees. There could be a hundred houses like this one hidden under the trees for all I know. For all anyone knows. Even so, when I first found the croft there was a rusty beer can, so I knew somebody else was here once, unless the ghosts that live here have a taste for cheap lager. Not that I believe in ghosts. There is no such thing as a soul. Nothing after we die. The girl in the lake could tell you that.

It is dark by the time I get back and my jeans are covered in mud from trying to find my way down the lane without a torch. I am afraid to go back into the caravan, but I'm not about to sleep in the barn just because of Doyle.

I try to go in quietly but the ill-fitting door and rusty metal step both squeal. They might as well be a burglar alarm, but inside the van is silent. Doyle's bedroom door is shut. I creep up to it, putting my ear slowly to the thin panel of the door.

'Doyle?' I whisper. 'You awake?'

'I am now.'

'Are you okay?'

'Get t' bed, for fuck's sake.'

I can't sleep. I'm still wound up and my midge bites are itching something fierce, so I lie in my bed listening to heavy drops falling from the trees above and hitting the metal roof like ball-bearings. The kitchen tap, dripping softly into the steel sink, echoes the tapping on the roof.

I'm still awake when Doyle gets up for a slash. He's thick-set and heavy but he treads lightly. Even so, the van's old floor panels groan under his weight and the door squeals against its frame. I listen to his piss hitting the grass outside. A moment later there is a brief flare in the darkness as he lights a fag. The night air carries a chilling wave of dampness through the caravan, bringing first smell of wet pine and bracken and then the smell of Doyle's fag.

'Doyle?'

'What?'

'I'm sorry about what I called you. I didn't mean it.'

'It doesn't matter. I get mouthy after a drink. Get to sleep.'

I pull the thin sleeping bag tighter around me. I feel better for a while, but when I close my eyes I dream of the girl. The bloating from the water has made her look fatter than she had been in life, so she is almost unrecognisable. Her skin is greasy looking, and taut, as though it might split. The water is dark and she is so white she seems almost to glow in the gloom beneath the trees. Not like when I'd see her working at the chippy; always hot and pink, sweat glistening in her cleavage.

When I wake, Doyle is standing in his y-fronts, pouring beans from a catering-size tin into a pan. 'Beans.' he says, and drops a bowl on the table as I slump into the seat. Instead of sitting down opposite me, he perches his old carcass on the counter, his crotch level with my face while I am trying to eat. As he gobbles his food out of the pan I can see his cock bobbing under the ancient fabric of his pants.

'Not hungry?'

'No. I'll have mine later. Ta though.'

'Watching your weight, eh?'

He lets out a long, disinterested fart before going back into the bedroom to get dressed.

Before Doyle comes out of his room I hear the sound of Pavel's clattering truck in the lane. He doesn't come out this way often. He must be here to see us, the lane doesn't go anywhere else, but I still jump when he bangs on the door. By the time I open it he is already staring impatiently through the kitchen window. I lean around the door frame and he turns to face me, picking mud from his overalls as he speaks.

'Why don't you answer your phones. It's a pain in my arse driving up here.'

'No signal,' I lie.

'I've got signal. Why haven't you?'

Doyle appears at my shoulder smelling of booze and cheap soap. 'Pavel, my friend. What can we do for you sir?'

'The road around the loch is off limits.'

'Oh, and why might that be?'

'Police. Doing something.'

'What?'

'The work crew found something.'

My mouth is going dry. 'I wonder if it's those townies have been up to something.'

Pavel looks at me like I'm an idiot. 'Townies? Why would they be there?'

'I bet it's them.'

'Bet what's them?'

'Whatever it is…'

'Whatever… I just came to tell you, stay out of the way. They will be up to see you, soon I think.'

'Us? Why us?'

'They question all the workers. Okay. See you. Goodbye.'

As Pavel starts his engine, Doyle waves him off and closes the door. 'Wanker.' He takes a beer from the fridge and starts guzzling it. 'Well now, that's interesting isn't it?'

'I suppose so.' I shrug, trying to look as though I don't care. He sits opposite me at the little table. I have the sudden sense he knows what is in the water, that he's known all along, that he's been playing with me.

'You been up at the loch recently?' He leans forward, too interested in my reply for me to be comfortable. I feel my face reddening.

'No. Why'd you say that?'

'No reason.'

'Why ask then?'

'Just curious.'

'Have you?'

'What?'

'Been up there?'

'What's it to you?'

He has been there, I can tell. He's making too much eye contact. The shifty bastard never looks you in the eye unless he's up to something or trying to psych you out.

'Thought you might know what it's all about.'

'No. Why would I?'

'I just thought…'

Doyle has a slight smile on his face. 'Sure there isn't something you want to tell me?'

Outside, I hear the sound of a car approaching slowly down the lane, crunching over the gravel and splashing through the puddles. I can tell by the engine it isn't Pavel's clapped-out truck. Doyle can't help himself, his eyes flicker towards the window. I see him swallow hard. They're not going to care what happened. They will just need someone to pin it on. They're coming for one of us.

I'm sweating now.

I need to get a grip. I take a long slow breath, flatten my voice and look him right in the eye. 'Doyle..?'

'What?'

'You never told me what you were inside for.'

He pauses mid gulp, a breathy burp hissing into the half-empty tin. There is a long silence while we stare at each other across a mile of sticky Formica. The morning sun bleeds through the mildewed, orange fabric of the curtain bathing everything in a deep, warm light and catching Doyle's eyes as he squints at me. I guess he's trying to remember what he's got on me, and wondering what I've got on him. Slowly he puts his beer down. 'Tell me again about all these townies that have been coming up here making trouble…'

Ray French

Voyager

Lynne started going to a new playground in another part of town, thirty minutes' walk from where she lived – daily exercise was one of the things on her list. It was spring, edging into summer, the days were longer and brighter, warmer, a good time to push herself more. She'd checked out a few other playgrounds, almost settled for one in a little park in Maindee, but the first time she saw this one it felt right. No-one knew her there, or anyone like her. Unless they had a cleaner. It was in the hilly part of town, the roads were steep and wide and she'd noticed how none of the trees had any branches torn off. The people who lived there were the kind who drove to Cardiff to do their weekly shop in Waitrose and read the posh papers, knew how to get their kids into good schools. No one looked twice at a dog walker. When she suggested it Alan agreed straight away.

'Now you're talking – there's nothing like a dog to keep you fit. And *you* won't mind, will you Buster? He'd never say no to a walk, would you boy?'

Buster was a big goofy old thing that looked like Scooby Doo. She wouldn't have had the nerve to do it without Buster.

Lynne stopped to catch her breath, and squinted down at the town. The civic centre, the clock tower and St Woolos, beyond that the Transporter Bridge, the putty coloured banks of the Usk glinting in the sun. It all looked so different from up there; flattened, grey, not quite real.

There was a sign that said no dogs in the playground, so she and Buster sat outside. She watched the mothers chatting nicely to each other. No effing and blinding, no slagging off the ones who weren't there. But then it was easy to be nice to people if you weren't worrying about money all the time. There were cliques though, there always were. Lynne soon picked out the inner circle – their accents were posher, less Welsh, their buggies and pushchairs probably cost as much as her neighbour's car. She saw the strain on the faces of the hangers on, how much they longed to move up the pecking order.

Lynne pretended to be looking something up on her phone, or she'd bring a paper. There was usually nothing but bad news so she started doing the crosswords, it gave her brain a work out and allowed her to look up more often, as if she was trying to figure out a clue. She was careful to come at different times each day. She'd have made a good spy, she'd missed her calling.

But in the end all she really needed was Buster, she was only being so cautious after what happened at the last playground. He lay at her feet, panting and would cock his head and stare at any child who came to the fence to smile. It was never long before the mother appeared.

'Is it okay if my little one comes and says hello to your dog?'

'Yes, of course, Buster loves kids.'

It never ceased to amaze her – if you had a friendly dog people trusted you. When Alan asked where she took Buster she'd said, 'Oh, all over' and he'd nodded, then asked if she wanted a cuppa and she'd relaxed.

Listening to the nicely spoken mothers, the children's voices, their laughter, the sheer joy on their faces as they petted Buster and he rolled over and let them tickle his belly made her happy, then sad, and then, after she'd been there a few times, hopeful. It scared her at first, it had been such a long time since she'd felt hopeful. She'd tried to fight it, like the craving for a drink. Then tried following Alan's advice and kept telling herself she deserved a break. Maybe he was right.

If you tell yourself something over and over, in the end you'll believe it.

He could drive you mad with his brilliant advice, her Uncle Alan, a lot of it was barmy, but every now and then he got something right. So she allowed herself to feel hopeful, watching those kids who were well taken care of, who looked healthy and confident and loved, and found that nothing else in the day came close.

You're pathetic, you are.

What choice did I have?

I don't know how you could live with yourself, doing something like that.

You think it was easy, what was I supposed to do?

Most of the conversations Lynne had these days took place in her head. She'd get furious, burst out crying or start laughing when she was in the middle of a blazing row with herself in the kitchen, or walking through the park, once when she was in Tesco's. When she'd noticed people staring she put down her basket and walked out. She waited then went back just before closing. There were new people on the tills, so she chose a sad-looking woman in her sixties at the one for 9 items or less. From the stiff way she held herself Lynne guessed there was something wrong with her back or shoulders. Arthritis, or maybe she'd had some kind of accident. Lynne hadn't wanted to say a word to anyone, just grab her shopping and get out of there as quickly as possible. It was a dismal place to find yourself at five to ten on a Saturday night, but the woman wanted to talk.

'The supermarkets are very convenient if you ever forget something, aren't they?'

She was Irish. They were talkers, the Irish. Lynne had Irish cousins, she liked them, they made her laugh – *that's grand, grand now, sure that's grand* – but they never shut up. They could never stand to live on her own, like her.

Well you soon ended up talking to yourself, didn't you?

'Sure we all forget things, don't we?'

Lynne couldn't just nod, or mutter 'mmm', pay for her things and walk away, couldn't.

'Yeah, I'm always forgetting things, me.'

'Oh you're not the only one, I'd lose my head if it wasn't screwed on.'

The woman was delighted, they'd hit it off, she'd made a new friend. Lynne wondered if she'd taken the job so she'd have people to talk to. She probably lived on her own, hardly ever spoke to anyone. Microwave meals in front of the telly. A couple of quid on the lottery at the weekend. A phone call once a week from a daughter in Cork or Kerry. On the way out she imagined Bridget (she looked like a Bridget), waiting at a bus stop, getting more frightened as the minutes passed and no bus came and the drunks and chavs milled around her, shouting and swearing. She couldn't bear the thought of it. She'd walk with her to the bus station, stay with her until her bus came.

Then she snapped out of it. Caught herself just in time. She knew exactly what she was doing. Like the time she nearly cried over the dog a couple of months before, when she'd first started jogging. After a few minutes she'd staggered to a tree, leant against the trunk, panting and wheezing as if she'd just completed a marathon.

Don't let the negative thoughts in. You've started something. It's all uphill from now on.

She was going to build up her self-esteem or

bloody die in the attempt. Lynne Hopkins the self-starter. She was open for business.

Listen to yourself, you silly cow.

An old bloke, he must have been in his 70s, was walking his dog on the rec. His mangy mongrel shuffled along behind him. It was wearing a bright pink collar with a big heart shaped disc hanging from it: there was something wrong with its back legs, they were twisted. The front half of the dog was trying to walk straight and the back half was trying to head for the road. Lynne nearly cried thinking how the poor little mite must get some terrible stick from all the Alsatians and Staffies. She watched the old twisted dog trying to follow its owner, going forwards, sideways, forwards, sideways. The man turned around and said, 'Come on, Delilah.'

Delilah. For Christ's sake.

She forced herself to look away, knew she'd end up seeing that crooked walk all day and start crying about the poor bendy-legged mongrel with the bright pink collar and the dangling heart the other dogs laughed at.

Delilah, the boy with the bright red birthmark on his face avoiding everyone's eyes in the post office, poor old Huw Edwards, who looked so heartbroken having to read yet more bad news and was putting on weight, obviously stuffing himself with comfort food late at night, there was a whole list of people and animals Lynne worried about. Now she was adding Bridget to it. Lynne made herself admit what she was doing – feeling sorry for someone else so she wouldn't have to face up to her own stuff. She wouldn't lie to herself, not any more. The truth was she only had Alan to talk to, and sometimes she couldn't take his positive outlook. It never stopped, he was like a puppy, or a born again Christian. She knew he meant well, god knows he had his own problems, but still. Sometimes you needed to say you felt like shit and not have the other person rush to try and make you feel better. Sometimes you just wanted them to listen. No, Lynne wasn't going to waste any more time worrying about other people, she needed to take care of herself.

She knew she'd head straight for Bridget the next time she went to Tescos.

The hardest thing she'd ever done, giving up the booze. The worst time had been early in the morning, when she woke and it was still dark. Unknown territory for years. Drink and early rising didn't go together. The booze kept her pinned to the bed, brimming with self-pity and loathing, till she eventually dragged herself up by afternoon, feeling like a zombie. She'd forgotten what it was like to wake that early, she'd bloody hated the winter months. At night there was the telly, music, things to do around the house – it was spotless these days – but she never felt more alone than when she woke up in the dark. On her own in the flat every sound was louder, harsher, unforgiving. She put the carrier bags down on the table – bang, it sounded like a pile of bricks. The kettle boiling was gravel churning in a mixer. Lynne was out of it for most of her twenties, half her thirties. Drink kept the world at a distance, anaesthetized her. Now she felt raw, exposed.

Sometimes she'd hear the couple above screwing and get up, get dressed, go outside and walk the streets till they'd finished. She'd hear them arguing, and wished she had someone she could call a fucking bastard and chuck things at, anything would be better than the loneliness. In the worst years with Dave she used to dream of escaping, running away from it all, living in her own place. The peace and quiet. No-one to bother her. Get things in perspective. Now she had a flat to herself and she hated it.

No, she didn't. Lynne wouldn't allow herself to think like that. Ruin the thing she'd craved for so long. Too easy. Now she was living on her own, she could start planning her future and there was no one to put her down, keep telling her she was stupid.

She got books out from the children's library and practised reading them aloud. *The Enormous Crocodile*, *We're Going on a Bear Hunt*, *Dogger*. Sometimes she'd burst into tears and fling the book on the floor. But she would get a grip, pick it up, and start again. *The Owl Who Was Afraid of the Dark*, *The Story of Babar, the Little Elephant*. She read them all, over and over and over again. Lynne learnt to pause, smile, whisper, deepen her voice and speed up in the right places, until she stopped feeling ridiculous and it began to come naturally.

Writing those lists had helped get her back on her feet. She'd made loads on her phone. The first one terrified her, there were so many things on it.

No more booze. Ever.

No more spliffs.

Eat healthy.

Daily exercise.

Get a job.

Take up yoga.

Make new friends, meet normal people.

Get a pet.

Go to Job Centre.

Ring mam.

Make it up with your sister.

On and on it went. Too much. Too many ways to fail and make herself miserable, give up, hit the drink again. She deleted it, wrote a new one. Kept it down to 5. 5 was a good number, she could cope with doing 5 things a day. 5 had a ring to it, 5 portions of fruit and vegetables a day. 5 things not to do on a first date. She decided to start with practical tasks – keep the kitchen clean, wipe down the cooker and surfaces. Do not put Sort Your Life Out as number 1. She tried again.

Clean the kitchen and keep it clean.

Eat healthy.

Do exercise.

Borrow one of Alan's relaxation tapes and try it.

Ring mam.

That was enough to be going on with. Ringing her mother and asking her – that would be the big one. But she didn't need to do that the first time they spoke, she could build up to it.

The lists had definitely helped. So did the light, now it was spring she'd wake before six and it wasn't dark. She'd hate to live in Scandinavia, she'd have drunk herself to death by now. The light and the lists and the hope had saved her.

She'd got the idea of making lists after Alan told her about Voyager 1. The Americans launched it back in 1977, and it was still out there shooting through space, travelling on and on into the unknown. There was a golden disc on board – they thought if Aliens heard it they'd get an idea of what our life on earth was like. There was all kinds of stuff on it: classical music, a song by pygmies, and a wedding song from Peru. The one that really got to her was 'Dark Was The Night', by Blind Willie Johnson. It was a very old recording, you could hear the scratches and the hisses. Willie played the bottleneck slide guitar, hummed and moaned, cried like a man on Death Row, and sang "I, I, I… Lord," but never finishing whatever he meant to say. That song was still out there, millions of miles away, no way of knowing if anyone would ever hear it. Lynne wondered what they'd think if they did?

Alan loved that song, he played it over and over. He said, 'That's what it felt like when I tried to give up drink the first time.'

The gold disc also included the sounds of a heartbeat, laughter, a dog, a horse and cart, Morse code. Lynne wondered what things she'd choose to send into space, if she wanted to let others know what her life was like?

A drunk trying to speak.

A woman crying.

The sound of a slap.

Someone saying I love you.

A mother talking to her baby.

He loved space, did Alan, the thought of it never ending. He had a map of the solar system on his bedroom ceiling, the stars had some kind of special cells, they glowed when he turned out the lights. She remembered when he'd first shown her. The two of them lay on his bed in the dark – that felt weird – she'd loved it when they lit up.

'Magic, innit?'

It was. Alan turned to her and said, 'Do you know what I'd be if I had my time again?'

'What?'

'An astronomer.'

Lynne knew not to laugh. She was glad she hadn't, god love him, the look on his face when he said it. Everyone else had been disgusted with her, gave up trying, even her parents. But not Alan. He'd been there, had the tee shirt. He never judged her, not once. She couldn't have come through it without him.

She hated blaming him, but neither of her parents were alcoholics, and she must have got it from someone.

Gradually she got healthier, put on weight, all those chocolates and puddings she treated herself to for persisting with the muesli, fruit and greens. She realised she was looking better when she'd walked past The Greyhound one day and a couple of blokes nodded at her. Hoodies, faded sweatshirts, baggy jeans. Raw drinkers' faces. Another ten years they'd be bloated, slurring their words. One of them, she knew him from somewhere, said 'How're you doing, Lynne?' He had a quite a few teeth missing. She walked on.

'Hey, what's the matter? Too good for us now, is it?'

She couldn't remember who they were, but knew she didn't want to know them now. It had been hard enough getting this far. They hated her for getting her act together. Wanted to drag her back down. She began to walk faster. It shook her up, the state of them. Had *she* looked that bad? What did they know about her? Had they seen her and Dave staggering home, yelling at each other? Watched her throw up in the gutter, or sliding down a wall, bawling her eyes out? They'd been the kind of people you saw on those TV programmes – *Britain's Worst Town Centres*.

The way the gummy one looked at her made her uncomfortable. It was another couple of hundred yards before it sunk in, it had been such a long time since anyone had looked at her in *that* way. Then she remembered his name – Garry, or Gazza, something like that. She'd sooner screw the homeless bloke who sat next to the cash machine outside the Spar in Tredegar Street. She tried to see it as a good sign – she was looking better, tried to imagine someone nicer than Garry looking at her in that way. But no, it didn't work, she wasn't sure she was ready for that yet, and all she saw was Garry's ravaged face, leering at her.

She'd gone to the first playground for a couple of months. She'd sat on a bench outside and pretend to be on her phone. She thought of it as revision. She'd no real memories left of playing with Catrin. It hurt watching those kids enjoying themselves. Some of the mothers, Jesus, she didn't want to go there, knew it wasn't fair, but she thought they didn't deserve them. Yapping away on their mobiles – *He's doing my head in, he's been a right little sod all day, he has* – fag in hand, effing and blinding. She wanted to rush over and hug their kiddies when they cried or looked lost.

But maybe she'd been no different. Probably she was worse. There was one little girl who was so lovely. You could see straight away she had a sweet nature, but her mother was a right hard-faced bitch, never paid her any attention, always on her mobile or filing her nails. One day, she must have been watching the girl too long, the mother started yelling at her.

'Hey you!'

She looked round, there was no-one else there. Then she looked back at the woman, she was getting up from the bench and walking towards her.

'You – I'm talking to you.'

Her face was red, spiteful. She *liked* being angry. The kind of woman who wouldn't think twice about going for you.

'What are you looking at?'

Suddenly there were no other voices, no birds singing, the ice cream van playing Greensleeves had fallen silent. She didn't remember getting up and leaving, but the next thing she knew she was walking down a street, light-headed, shaken, her legs rubbery as if she were coming down with the flu. She sat down on someone's doorstep and hugged herself. For a minute or two she thought she'd faint, lowered her head and held onto the step. The door opened behind her.

'Are you alright, love?'

A woman's voice, elderly. Someone with kids her age. No, grandkids.

'Do you need a doctor?'

The woman sounded so kind Lynne wanted to cry. She daren't answer, what could she say?

I wasn't going to snatch her kid.

No, not a good opening line.

'Ring her,' Alan said, 'You know you have to.'

'I'm not ready.'

'You never will be, love. You just have to do it.'

They were walking Buster on the rec. Now the weather was warmer Alan was dressed in that awful shirt with the palm trees and the surfers gliding on waves he'd got in the Help The Aged charity shop, a pair of white plastic sunglasses with thick frames. He looked like someone going mental in the community. He hummed as they walked. He was a great hummer these days, Alan. He hummed and he chewed gum, kept offering it to her even though she shook her head every time. Lynne had given up telling him she didn't like it. Alan the mad hummer – *Men of Harlech* segued into *Whole Lotta Love*, then, as they walked across the rec and felt the sun on their faces, he moved on to *It's A Beautiful World*. Some days it was too much, but she knew he couldn't help it, it was his way of coping. Everyone had their ways.

'Let's do it now. I'll be here, next to you.'

Lynne stopped, took a deep breath. Alan squeezed her hand.

'Lynne, she's my sister, I know what she's like. Putting it off won't help. It'll never get any easier. Come on, let's do it.'

The night before she'd looked at the photos of Catrin her mother had sent. She was 4 now, she would be starting school in Porthcawl in September. It was too late.

'She won't remember me.'

'Don't talk daft. You're her mother.

You're not fit to have her. The state I found her in, thank god I came when I did, and you passed out on the floor in the bathroom. She's better off with us.

She felt her legs going.

Alan sat her down on a bench.

'She'll be in now. They'll have had their lunch, she'll be sitting down and reading the paper, Ron will be in the garden.'

He was right, it would never get any easier. Her heart raced when her mother picked up the phone. She couldn't speak.

'Hello, who is this?'

Lynne's throat tightened.

'Hello?'

'Mam, it was a year yesterday since I had a drink.'

There was a long, charged silence.

'That's good.'

Lynne was furious. Her mother was frightened, she could tell. But Christ, she deserved more than that. In the background she heard her father say, 'Who's that, Helen?' Then, 'Are you alright?' She could picture her mother, rigid, gripping the telephone lead, shooting him a warning look.

Alan was whispering, 'Ask her.'

The silence stretched on.

'Mam…'

Her dad would be backing out of the hall now, sensing bad news, and not wanting to get involved. Putting the kettle on for when it was over.

'Mam, I want to come and see Catrin.'

There was a long sigh.

'Mam?'

'This is not a good time, Lynne. Me and your father are just about to go out. Let's talk about this some other time. I've got to go now. Bye bye.'

She put the phone down. Alan grabbed her, pulled her into his chest and held on while she went limp.

'You did it, Lynne love, you did it. You took the first step. Come on, let's have a cuppa.'

One of the mothers from the inner circle was watching her little boy rub Buster's head. The look on his face, the sheer joy, Lynne could have watched him all day. She realised the mother was talking to her.

'Sorry, what was that?'

The mother was pretty, and knew it. Her thick black hair was slicked back with a claw clip, she had one of those thick leather hairbands that were popular years ago, must be back in fashion again. She was looking at Lynne curiously.

'I said, do you have any kids yourself?'

Lynne felt caught out, trapped. Then the pretty mother leant down and rubbed Buster's head and said, 'Tom would love a dog, but it's such a responsibility, isn't it? What do you do when you go on holidays, do you put him in kennels?'

Lynne almost laughed, a holiday, that would be nice. But the woman was probably only trying to be friendly.

'I take him with me, I couldn't bear to leave him behind.'

'Aaaw, he's a big softy, isn't he?'

She took her son's hand.

'Come on then, Tom, let's leave the lady in peace.'

As they turned to go, Lynne said, 'I have a daughter, she's four.'

N. Jane Kalu

To Have a Ghost Baby

It means your eyes carry bags so heavy your face drops to the floor. Ghost babies never sleep. They let out continuous screams loud enough to penetrate concrete walls. They will eat nothing. They will listen to no lullaby. They do not lie still in their cots but move around the house at will. Sometimes only you can hear it. Even when you decide to ignore it, a big pillow over your head doesn't muffle out the shrill. Of course, it's not just your eyes that droop towards the floor but your entire 40-year-old body. It is as though the wooden floor of your two-story house is a magnet, and you are made of steel. It becomes tough to lift your feet, to move your lips, to even breathe in the smell of Lagos' first rain outside the window. At first, your husband is helpful. He buys ear plugs, then one of those white noise producing things. He carries you in his arms, plans a night with candles and jollof rice on the dining table, scented candles in the bathroom, scented candles in the bedroom, but he doesn't understand what it means to have a ghost baby.

You somehow knew, always suspected. Your right palm was glued to your bump the whole nine months. You rubbed, listened. There was that one time, right in the middle of the day, while watching Tinsel, that you touched your bump and it spoke to you. I am a ghost baby, it said. You jumped out of the couch, asked it to say it again, but it didn't need to, it was embedded in your brain now. You made positive affirmations as your mother's pastor instructed, saying over and over again —a ghost baby is not my portion. But like a festering wound attracts houseflies, you now saw a ghost baby being handed out everywhere you looked. It was there on your Facebook timeline, on the Expectant Mothers' thread, on the front page of the Newspapers street vendors shove at your window in slow traffic. It was there at the hospital when you went for antenatal. Let's not even get started with those hospital visits. All you did was lie there and study, not the monitor, but the doctor's expressions. While rubbing pink gooey jelly all over your belly with that probe stick thingy, the doctor, like something rehearsed, went from frowning, to creasing his eyebrows, to a straight face, and then, a smile, while he peered at the monitor. It was the smile you paid attention to. Was it a smile of pity, or was it the I'm-so-relieved-I-don't-have-to-announce-you're-having-a-ghost-baby kind? It was all a façade anyway, this studying of the doctor's face. Because even with the I'm-so-relieved-I-don't-have-to-announce-you're-having-a-ghost-baby smile you got every visit, you still got a ghost baby.

Nobody can tell you where ghost babies come from. The doctor dances around the subject. Medical science offers no explanation. Your mother turns out to be even more clueless than the doctor. She didn't get one, no woman in your family has, it's just you.

Nobody mentions the wild stories about ghost babies: how they go to the women who eat certain fruits or don't eat certain fruits, or to the women who expose their pregnant bellies and allow strangers to stroke them, to women who don't stay up at night shouting loud prayers that get their neighbors to fling open their windows and cuss at them. They don't tell you about how evil spirits can go deep into your ancestral lineage and fetch ghost babies out, or (finally, when all stories have been exhausted) how they go to people who are just unlucky in this world. You don't know which category you belong to, and you wish somebody would tell you. Your husband's family announces their disclaimer right at the hospital. They'd never had one, no woman in their family has ever had a ghost baby.

Maybe you got it because you are *Igbo,* ghost babies are not common amongst their tribe, they suggested, turning away their faces.

We will figure out how to take care of this, your mother promises. Him. The ghost baby is a boy, you want to remind her.

Everything will turn out alright, your mother says with the audacity that could only come from one who has no experience in these things.

You know more about this baby than she does, but you allow her to move into the guest room anyway. Getting a ghost baby means the walls are always closing in on you when the baby stops crying and you go from room to room searching for him. You need your mother.

The ghost baby makes everyone nervous. And not for the obvious reasons. It's those bags under your eyes. When the neighbors visit, their eyes dart from side to side as if looking for somewhere safe to set their gaze. And you, you sit there in that wicker chair, right across from them, rocking back and forth, and it's hard to tell if you're staring at them or through them. It's worse with the neighbors who have ghost babies of their own because they always say, it gets better. You glare at them, you want to ask them to take my screaming boy home please. You watch them dig into the sofa in their discomfort praying it will swallow them whole. You're easier on the ignorant neighbors. They show up with a bowl of *nsala* soup and chat about the boiling weather with your mother, or the economy with your husband, or try to talk to your dark eyes about the terrible Lagos traffic, and then they're out of there, almost running down the street back to their homes. Nobody asks to hold the ghost baby, to dance around the room with the ghost baby in their arms and perhaps help stop the screaming. Nobody asks what you've named him.

In the meantime, your mother takes care of the spiritual requirements prescribed for the circumstance. Prayers. Chants. Burning Incense. A frenetic dance you are pretty sure has nothing to do with the scriptures. You know she's gone back to her village in the east and seen a traditional priest. There are palm leaves dangling from the ceiling of your living room. You're not even sure why this needs to be done. You sit there on the couch next to your husband, with the ghost baby in your arms, and watch this ridiculousness. Your husband echoes the ritual responses, but you know he would rather be at a quiet bar in Lekki yelling at a soccer game with his office colleagues. He wants to take care of his ghost baby too, but like you, hasn't figured out what works. He thinks participating in the ritual will help. Soon, he will think leaving you alone will help.

There is a lot of movement in the house now. There's the ghost baby roaming the house. There's you following him. There's your mother following you. There's no space left for your husband. He enters the car and drives off. *Office,* he says. You take the screaming ghost baby in your arms and go for a walk. You know your mother won't follow you. She's worried about the parted blinds and curtains in the houses you walk by. She remains at the porch until you walk up to a front door and ask for paracetamol to help with your pounding head, and she dashes over to take you home.

My head aches, you almost yell at her.

At home she gives you ginger tea.

When the ghost baby is a few months old, after your mother returns to her house on the other side of Lagos, after the smell of new rain is gone and all that is left are wet walls and damp smells, after the movement stops and you lie in bed all day cuddling the ghost baby, you find a group of people who know how to care for ghost babies. Someone on your Expectant Mothers' thread recommended them. They meet in the living room of a nice Church sister, she typed. But it's a few weeks before you get in the car with the ghost baby strapped in the backseat. You'd searched for the car seat someone gave you at the shower but couldn't find it. You remembered your mother had put away some of those things because ghost babies don't need them anyway, and, you stood so long in the nursery staring at them you scared her. There are no regulations for ghost babies in vehicles. You could hold them in your lap while driving, strap them in the front seat, or just lay them there in the back seat. Nobody would care. Not even the police.

When you arrive at the meeting, the women welcome you with smiles and someone vacates their chair for you. You look from one face to the other, but you find their eyes bagless, and you start to look towards the door. Your skepticism only starts to melt when they show you their own ghost babies. One even has twin ghost babies. How do you cope with them, you ask her? She smiles. They all smile. Soon, you'll learn that smile, too.

By the time you're back in the car driving home, you've learned a few things:

The crying will stop.

The headaches will go away.

Ghost babies are obedient when they're older and will do whatever you ask of them.

Ghost babies become anything you want them to.

But before there's a chance for any of this to happen, your husband sleeps with a 20-year-old from the neighborhood. Women that age are at a low risk of having ghost babies. *Sorry,* your husband says, his head stuck out the window as he backs out of the driveway with three big suitcases in the trunk of his car. You stand at the porch and watch the car until it splashes the puddle at the end of the street. The blinds in the house across the street stretch open. You stare at the window until the blinds snap shut.

By the next morning, the ghost baby stops crying. He sits there in your lap sucking his fingers. It is in all that calmness that you finally see your ghost baby, first, a toddler, running around the house. You see him on a high school soccer team. You see him in the yard with his friends from the next street. You see him win a medal, graduate, get married. And you realize like human babies, he will stop coming to his mother so often. Listening to the sucking sound echoing in the empty house, you lean back in the wicker chair, and finally, you close your eyes.

Marylee MacDonald

Caboose

Sister Salina Limone didn't impose her views on other people. That was the fact of the matter, as anyone with half a brain could plainly see. At the end of the day, she came in to find dishes in the kitchen sink. She tidied up. That was all. Simple tidying up like any woman did. And, yes, she had carried Sister Mary Margaret's books and legal pads to the bedroom, but only because the living room, with its throw-covered futon and overstuffed chair, was where they invited their neighbors—hookers and crackheads and their kids—to come for soup and prayers. The children needed an island of sanity, as did she, and even though it might be the Christian thing to do, she didn't think visiting her father would make her a better roommate.

Sister Nearing held up a hand. "Take a breath, Sister Limone."

Salina hopped up. "Can I get you a drink?"

"No, thank you," Sister Nearing said.

A dead palm frond stuck in a framed picture of Jesus, cradling his Sacred Heart. Salina plucked off the frond, crumpled it, and put it in the pocket of her denim skirt.

"Come sit a moment and let's pray." Sister Nearing, the Director of the Mid-Atlantic region, patted the futon.

Salina pulled a chair from the drop-leaf table. Swinging her leg over the seat, she sat backwards and rested her chin on her fingers.

Sister Nearing rubbed the back of her neck. "Let us be mindful of Our Lord's charity."

Salina bowed her head. A motorcycle revved in the parking lot. One of the pimps. Above her head, rhythmic thuds rattled the light. Jorge and his basketball. Salina crossed herself.

"Sister Mary Margaret's not cut out to live with poor folk," Salina said.

"I hope you're wrong about that."

"I might be wrong about a lot of things, but not about that."

She slid off the chair and went to the window. Pulling back the curtains, she looked out to the parking lot and saw Jorge, eleven and just beginning to grow a mustache, hopping on the bike he'd stolen. Opening the door was the signal he could come up for snacks. Apples, oranges, not the things that appealed to him, but sometimes he came up anyway.

"I think we need some fresh air."

"Can't you stop pacing?"

Salina opened the door, backed against the wall, and crossed her arms.

"I guess you must be wondering why I drove all this way when a phone call would have sufficed," Sister Nearing said.

"You're going to kick me out."

"Is that why you're so defensive?"

"I have as much right to live here as they do."

"You think I'm going to kick you out?"

"It's two against one."

"Sister Mary Margaret only wants what's best for you."

"I know what's best for me."

Sister Nearing made a steeple of her fingers. "Your repetitive behaviors get on her nerves."

"She wants to mess with my head," Salina said.

"It's not just Mary Margaret," the Director said. "Sister Klanac finds your behavior annoying, too."

Fat Sister Klanac? *Lazy* Sister Klanac, the Croatian who didn't eat enough at the bakery but had to stick a bag of popcorn in the microwave the instant she came home?

"I could complain about her if I wanted," Salina said. "She leaves the lights on. She runs up the electricity."

The Director sighed. "Sister Klanak says you're always jumping up to wipe the counter, even during dinner. If someone drops a fork, you're faster than a busboy."

"It's hard for her to bend over."

"Is that why you get out the dust mop and make a point of dusting around her feet?"

"She drops popcorn on the floor."

"But you make her nervous," the Director said, her voice rising. "Can't you see that it makes people nervous if you're constantly in motion?"

"I can't help it." Behind her back Salina twisted the doorknob. Where was Jorge when she needed him? She spun around and went out onto the balcony. The parking lot was full of cars with sagging bumpers and broken windows. She came back in and shut the door. "I don't like to sit."

The Director opened her briefcase and removed a manila folder. "A year ago you said your father was getting on in years, and at some point, you'd like to take care of him. Has that time come?"

Salina's chest felt tight. She ran her fingers through her close-cropped hair. The last time she'd seen him, her hair had hung down to her hips. "I didn't say I'd like to take care of him. I said I might have to."

Standing, the Director put her folder on the chair and reached for Salina's free hand, pulling her away from the wall. Sister Nearing's fingers felt cold. Her grip tightened.

Salina pulled free.

"Perhaps there is some unfinished business," Sister Nearing said, drawing near. "Something in your past?"

Salina took a step back. "There's not." She disliked anyone standing inside the invisible circle she drew around herself.

"A change of scene might do you good."

"Not that change of scene."

Once a person cut off communication, it was better to keep it cut off. She'd seen her dying clients mend fences with their families, and others try and fail. You could never really fix what went wrong in the past. Some things were so broken thcy could never be mended, and all that Kubler-Ross, death-and-dying talk only led to unrealistic expectations. Dying people needed their faces washed. They needed their butts wiped. They needed ice chips and swabbed tongues.

"Move me someplace else, then," Salina said.

Sister Nearing put the folder back in her briefcase. "I can't see any other options, Salina."

"I try to get along with people."

"You get along with your clients fine," Sister Nearing said. "It's just your roommates, which I don't really understand because, you know, we've had this conversation before."

Salina hung her head. "Maybe I should never have…"

"Let's not question your vocation." Sister Nearing. "It's an odd thing. You don't have a bad temper. You're hardworking and dedicated to the people we're trying to serve. You've found your ministry in home health care. In all these ways the Sisters of Mercy fit you well. For the life of me, I can't figure out what's at the root of this."

"Nothing is at the root of it," Salina said, arms crossed and pacing.

Sister Nearing smiled. "Ever since I met you, you've struck me as a very old soul."

"What's that mean?"

"Those black eyes of yours..."

"I'm Mexican!" Salina said.

"Don't take offense."

"I just like to stay busy," Salina said.

"What would you think about if you sat down?" Sister said. "Perhaps there's some, uh, abuse in your background? Something you've been reluctant to share?"

A wave of heat washed over Salina's head, like in the shower, with the water ten degrees too hot. There was no abuse, not sexual, if that's what Sister Nearing meant, and as for how she was raised, well, that was her business. She'd told them all they needed to know.

"What is it you want?" Sister Nearing said.

"I want everyone to leave me alone."

"Then, go home, Sister Limone."

"For how long?"

"Two weeks, let's say. A month?"

"Hospice won't let me have that much time off."

"I'll see what I can do."

"But will I have to come back here?"

"I don't have another alternative," Sister Nearing said. "We live in community, Sister Limone."

"I know, I know."

"What do you say?"

Two weeks off. Maybe a month. Could she bear it?

"I'm not exactly sure where my father lives."

"What does he do?"

"Odd jobs for ranchers."

"Give me the information, and I'll call the Bishop. Maybe reconnecting with him will bring you some peace."

"I doubt it," Salina said.

"Why's that?" Sister Nearing said.

"Because I'll have to figure out a place to stay."

"Can't you stay with your father?"

"No," Salina said.

"Is he homeless?"

"It's a rural area. Let's just say hogs lived better."

"I see," Sister Nearing said. "Well, let's make sure there's someone to meet you. What airport would you fly into? Denver?"

"I'll take the bus," Salina said.

"Are you afraid of flying?"

"I just need time to make a transition."

#

Weary from the eighteen-hour trip from Washington D.C., Salina huddled against the Greyhound's rain-spotted window. She'd managed to sleep through the toilet opening and slamming shut, but as the bus hopscotched from town to town, the smell of chemicals had woken her up. Now, holding a handkerchief over her nose, she checked her cell phone to see if it miraculously had service. Fallow fields stretched to the horizon. Some deacon was supposed to pick her up.

The bus pulled into the station. In a line of passengers waiting to board the bus, she saw a man holding a sign. NUN MOBILE. A black Stetson covered his dome-of-a-head, and he wore cowboy boots and a bolo tie. In all her time out east, she'd forgotten bolo ties.

His eyes ran up and down her sweatshirt and jeans. "Dr. Francis Clancy, at your service."

"Doctor?"

"Actually, a vet. Large animal. It's 'Doc' to my

friends."

"Am I your friend?"

"Sure. Why not?"

The driver took suitcases from the luggage compartment.

"Which one is yours?" Doc said.

"The pink vinyl."

"The one with Cinderella decals?"

"That's the one."

"But it's a kid's suitcase."

"I'm short."

"Suit yourself."

"I found it in an alley."

"Oh ho! Chip off the old block."

What was that supposed to mean? She didn't like people who presumed to know her business. The trip had worn her down, and now, on top of seeing her father, she had to deal with this deacon fellow.

He gave the driver a dollar bill and waited in the lobby while she used the restroom. Then he was driving east, and she took out her rosary and fingered the beads. Eventually he took the exit to a state route, and then a county road lined by crooked wooden fence posts strung with barbed wire. The parched grass and clumps of windblown trees signaled yet another rural, Colorado town, the one she recognized as her father's mailing address. There was a barbershop with a red-white-and-blue barber's pole mounted on the wall. She imagined him fortyish, in a straw hat, cowboy boots, and ranch jeans, a short, wiry Mexican with a weathered face, thin mustache, and gold tooth. But, of course, he would have aged.

The town's small brick post office had a picture window, but its shade was drawn down. Somehow she had expected him to be sitting outside on its empty bench, waiting the way he waited to catch a ride with whomever might be heading out to wherever he worked.

The deacon turned into a gravel drive. A hundred feet back from the road sat a white, clapboard building the size of a one-room school, St. Mary's Catholic Church.

She got out of the car.

He brought her suitcase. "Let me show you the church."

"Is my father going to meet us here?"

"He died yesterday."

The ground fell from beneath her feet. "How could that be?"

"He's been sick for some time."

"With what?"

"Old age."

She looked past the church. A few brick houses with small, fenced yards sat among the trees. An Airstream trailer gleamed in the light of the rising moon.

Speechless, she stood there shaking and hoping the tremble would stop so she could take a step forward. Go see the church, or whatever it was he expected her to do.

"Now what?"

"There'll be a service. We figured you'd want to plan it."

"Yes, yes, of course," she said. "But, I came all this way to see him."

"Well, I know he would have been glad to see you, to see any of his kids for that matter. But I understand. Busy with your own lives. Scattered all over kingdom come."

He walked to the back door of the church. "See

here? Just last week, Hugo put a fresh coat of paint on the church steps."

He took a key from a nail under the top step, and she saw that, yes, the back steps were covered with a slick, gray coat of paint, evidence of her father's recent life.

"Where am I to stay?"

"Here. I made up a cot."

"Is there a shower?"

"No, but there's running water and a toilet."

The deacon unlocked a door and led her into a small room that doubled as an office and a dressing room. Below the window was an Army cot, a camping mattress, and folded blankets.

"This be okay?" he said.

"I've slept in worse."

The deacon fiddled with the thermostat. A gush of heat came from the floor grate.

An old wooden desk of the schoolteacher variety stood in the corner, its desk chair rocked back as if someone had recently been sitting in it. A priest's white chasuble hung in an open wardrobe.

"Who says mass?" she said.

"Once a month Father Rodriguez comes out from La Junta."

"La Junta."

"Been there?"

"We lived there."

"It figures."

"What do you mean?"

"There's a lot of Mexicans."

This deacon fellow was getting on her nerves.

"Does Father Ramirez speak Spanish?"

"Enough to get by."

Through the door that opened into the nave, she

saw two rows of pews, thirty rows in all. This was where her father would have prayed.

The deacon turned on the light. She slid into the second row and flipped down a kneeler. All the inchoate feelings about the way she'd grown up, the things that had propelled her and held her back, came at her in a swirl. Now she understood why her clients were so eager to have that final, death-bed scene. Why they sought forgiveness.

#

Twenty years ago, her sister had brought their worn-out mother up to Wyoming, but their father, always with that far off look in his eyes, had refused to leave this blink-in-the-road he'd decided to call home. Manuela in Wyoming didn't want to take him on, and Olga, in Council Bluffs, said she had her hands full. Juan, who lived in a double-wide in San Bernardino, said, "Let him live in one of his crazy little houses." And, so now, Salina guessed, they had all demonstrated their heartlessness and lack of compassion, and the only thing to do was to pray for the soul of Hugo Limone. Slipping a rosary from her pocket, she fingered the beads.

Crossing herself, she sat back in the pew and looked at the tabernacle on the altar. The altar cloth needed starch. Dust covered the antique organ. It had probably been years since anyone played it. Tomorrow, she could clean this all up.

Dr. Clancy slid into the pew. His shoulders were shaking, and he had a handkerchief over his mouth.

She bowed, feeling ashamed, not so much that she'd missed saying goodbye, but that she couldn't match the deacon for being broken up. But, of course, he would be if he and her father were friends.

"How, exactly, did he die?"

"Well, ma'am, he laid down in a field and just expired."

"Did he freeze?"

"Not so's the Coroner could tell. Hugo had put on his Sunday suit—"

"He never had a Sunday suit—"

"—as if he'd a mind to call it quits."

"People don't just die when they want to," she said.

"Horses do," he said.

"Who's the Coroner?" she said.

"I am." His eyes crinkled in a squint. "I looked him over."

"Is this a joke?" she said. "Because the father I remember was quite the practical joker."

He patted her shoulder. "I wouldn't pull your leg on something like this."

"I'm still having trouble understanding how he could die. Usually people hang on, even after you think it's ridiculous."

"I reckon that's true."

"Did you tell me what he had? Was it bladder cancer? Leukemia? Something painful and untreatable?" A passing truck made the windows rattle. "Otherwise, I don't understand how he could be painting the steps one day, and then just walk out into a field and lie down with the intention to die the next."

She should call her roommate, Sister Mary Margaret, and ask if she could look up in her books why a man would take his own life. Maybe he just didn't want to be old. Or, was he as afraid of seeing her as she was of seeing him?

She took a tissue from her purse and dabbed her

eyes, wanting the deacon to think she felt more than she did. Mary Margaret was always probing with her ice pick mind. Feelings, Sister Salina. What are your feelings? And this was the thing, as she was seeing now for the very first time, she did not have feelings like other people. She pretended to blow her nose. Until she got back to D.C., she'd have to pretend to be shaken up and grieve, because that was the natural reaction.

"It sounds like you knew my father very well," she said.

"Oh, I do." He squint-smiled. "Did."

"How did you even communicate?"

"Pidgin English. What with my two hundred words of horse Spanish and his two hundred words of English, we got on fine. You should take a gander at where your father lived," he said. "He's got quite the setup."

"Let me get my bearings first."

"It's only a quarter mile from here and the walk'll do you good. It's just a shame you got here too late."

Yes, it was. It was ridiculous.

#

Concrete silos sat at the edge of town. At the end of the dead-end spur, she saw the Atchison, Topeka, and Santa Fe caboose, its paint not red, as she had imagined when Dr. Clancy described it, but the shocking turquoise of the Adriatic Sea. The last time she'd spoken to her father, he'd called from a pay phone. She'd asked him what was new. "Farmers bringing in winter wheat," he said in Spanish, but he had never told her about the caboose.

By the time she reached for the steel hand-grip and pulled herself onto the rear platform, her teeth chattered and her body ached. Nerves, probably. Inside, the beaded wainscoting that came half way up the walls reminded her of the kitchen at Robert Andresson's house. A gay man from Abilene, he shared her love of fourth of July parades and county fairs; she had walked him through the last six months of his life, and after that she'd told the order she needed a break and wanted a job in a nursing home. She wasn't Mother Teresa and what she couldn't take was letting herself get close to people and then letting go. Now, here she was dealing with death again, her father's death, when she had not sufficiently grieved Mister Andresson, humorous till the end. Those were the ones it was hardest to let go of, the ones who made you laugh, and she was dismayed to find these feelings still inside her, the deep ache of loss for a man who was not a blood relative.

On a table flanked by built-in benches sat an open box of Bicycle cards, the Jokers set aside, the game of solitaire half-played. She wondered if Dr. Clancy had ever come out here. Surely, if he had, there'd be bottles of bourbon or six packs of beer. In his younger days her father had enjoyed a drink, but never to excess, not like Sister Nearing probably thought.

Opposite the table stood a brown propane stove, a box of matches on the shelf above it. It had been fifty years since she'd seen a stove like that, but she remembered how her grade school teacher lit it. She knelt and flipped open a door and saw the knob that said, "Pilot." Expecting to blow herself up, she pressed the knob for thirty seconds. The match ignited a blue flame, and by the time the match burnt down to a small black worm, she had the burners on. She would just have a quick look around.

Across from the stove a narrow stair led up to a cupola that she had noticed in a glancing way. Now that she stood inside the caboose, looking up to the second story, a wave of bitterness swept through her, and she crossed herself to make it go away. After all these years her father had found a two-story house for himself, a place that must be tall enough for him to see the distant mountains as a sort of backdrop, the way an audience might see them in a play.

Four shallow, workmen's closets stood on one side of the hall, their narrow doors sticking as she pulled them open. Who was this man, this illiterate sweeper of grain elevators, this church janitor for the little parish of St. Mary's, where the steps and handrail had been carefully brush-stroked gray: his last day's work before his seemingly planned death, about which she had plenty of feelings, mainly shame.

#

Her father had been born in Morelia, Mexico. In 1942, he had come north to harvest sugar beets in Stockton, California. He had met Salina's mother, thirteen, a girl from a family of second-generation field workers. Salina had been told she was named for the Central Valley town that meant "salts." Whoever had registered her birth certificate had dropped the final "s". None of this she'd given a thought to until her father moved them to Colorado. He'd fallen out with a man at work. By then she was in fourth grade, struggling to catch up in math, but a good reader. She had lived there five years. At fourteen, hoping to get back to the sunshine and warm winters, she'd run away from home, if you could call where they lived home. She'd fought off a trucker, using the shiv her little brother gave her as a goodbye gift, and the trucker dumped her outside Kansas City. After that, she'd taken up with a Southern

Baptist, short-order cook who'd coaxed her into a full immersion baptism in the river, and it was the shame of letting herself be brainwashed into joining a congregation that heard voices and rolled on the floor that sent her east. Working in the kitchen at Mercy Hospital in Council Bluffs, Salina spent so many lunch hours in the chapel that Sister Mary Alma, head of Food Services, asked if something was wrong.

"I like to pray," Salina said. Prayer was the only thing that calmed her down.

"Have you ever considered a religious vocation?" Sister Mary Alma said.

"I'm not a virgin," Salina said.

"Your vow of chastity only begins after a period of reflection." Sister Mary Alma had taken her hand, and for the first time since Salina had left home, she felt a slight relaxation of the unkind words she'd called herself for leaving her mother with all those little kids and a quixotic, unreliable jokester.

#

He still lived in a boxcar, though one far fancier and more luxurious than the boxcar she'd lived in as a child. His caboose had a narrow bed with a two-inch mattress. Salina had expected the bed to have no sheets, but it had flowered sheets and an orange and pink comforter, the kind of thing women from the church might have given him. He had kicked the sheets down to the foot of the bed, the comforter, too, as if he'd had a restless night. The mattress itself had the old covered buttons and blue-and-white-striped ticking that she remembered from Italian sleeping cars, a luxury for the nuns going to Rome for the first time, and she recalled the rocking motion that lulled her to sleep and that woke her to the marvel of a tangerine sun, just as the train entered the Holy City.

As in all train cars, everything on the Italian train had been designed for efficiency: the metal sink that flipped down from a hidden cavity in the wall, the upper bunk that pulled down like a rumble seat, the bench that made a bed, and the reading light where she'd read Paul's "Letter to the Ephesians."

Here, too, in the home her father had created for himself, everything had its place. His worn overalls hung from a hook. She folded them to take back to town. Surely the church would have a clothes bin for the needy, though who could be needier than her father, she couldn't imagine. She would have to pick up some Woolite to wash his red flannel shirt; even a thrift shop wouldn't take dirty clothes. Across from the flannel shirt hung an undershirt whose underarms were the color of his wind-burnt face. In the small, silverless mirror hanging from a nail, she imagined him pulling aside the skin of his jaw to approve the face he showed to the world, for, though a short man, he had always been vain about his high cheekbones and the skin of a man twenty years younger.

#

At the front of the caboose she found the kitchen and a garbage bag half-full of empty cans. Her order hadn't allowed her to send him money. All her earnings went to a common fund. But whenever an employer or family member slipped her a twenty for some extra service—a fault of her compulsive tidying—she folded shirt-cardboard around the cash and sent it by mail, not even wanting the trail of a check because he'd never had a bank account and could only sign his name with his mark, something that looked more like a cattle brand than an H.

A single hot plate was connected by a cracked pink hose to a propane canister on the floor. This could very well be the same burner her mother had used to feed a family of six. Or, maybe it was a hot plate he'd found discarded in an alley.

Always looking for scraps of corrugated roofing, discarded boards, or half-used cans of paint, he spent Sundays after mass exploring. His walks took him through the alleys behind La Junta's neat grid of bungalows, the houses where the white people lived. And if it wasn't shameful enough that their only shelter was a boxcar, where everyone in town knew the Limone family lived, over the years an outhouse-sized subdivision of buildings grew up around it. Her father decorated each little structure with hub caps and parts of bumpers. Each dwelling had a small door and a window with a single pane of glass. Hers was painted barn red, her sister's the yellow of egg yolk. When she was small, she had been pleased to busy herself wiping the window and sweeping the floor, making believe it was a real house and hers alone. "If you want to be building these places for the children," Salina's mother had told him, "you should look for a third job." Hurt, he'd hopped down out of the box car, out of the chaos of toddlers and bickering brothers and Salina's endless rounds of blanket folding, sweeping, and changing the divisions of the fruit crates that made up the low, splintered walls of the children's half, and off he'd gone to drag more treasures home.

When she was young, the family's drinking water had come from an aluminum watering can of the kind farmers' wives used for their gardens. It sat by the boxcar's door, along with an aluminum cup. Here, though, he had a much nicer water container, a 3-gallon, Coleman camping thermos. She pushed a button to see if the water had frozen. It had not.

Of the cans stacked in a pyramid on a shelf, she saw peaches, apricots, *menudo*, and an 8-ounce can of Rosarita tamales. On the counter sat a white enamel wash bowl with a red rim, and in it, a plate with a dried brown crust and a dirty spoon, almost as if he had left it for her to wash up. The loaf of Wonder Bread in the bread box had not yet hardened. Squeezing it, she felt the freshness of his death and a collective shame for all his offspring, none of whom had made it to the funeral of the man whom this desolate parish, in its generosity, had honored with its care. It was too much to say he was beloved because she had not yet met the other parishioners and couldn't tell. Maybe it was more that he had carved out a tiny niche of work that he alone could do. He had made himself essential and, at the same time invisible, the way he had done when she was a child.

Her hands felt soiled. She pressed the water again and wiped her palms on her jeans. Gathering the cans, she carried them to his room. Heat from the stove had finally reached his nest. She took a deep breath to inhale whatever remnant of his smell remained. All old men had their odors. She likened it to cloves or chewing tobacco, and smelled the objects that had been close to him as she made her hobo's bundle. The only smell that called up a memory was a sliver of soap next to his razor. Fels-Naptha, a combination of moth balls and bay leaves, a smell she associated with her mother and the round steel tub in which she could clearly see her mother's hands working a shirt up and down on the corrugated washboard. No one used that soap nowadays. Fels-Naptha was for serious dirt—oil and black grease, or for the dirt embedded in the knees of overalls. It was the soap for a man who'd spent his life close to the ground and the soap for Salina's mother, whose life's constant struggle was to make her children not look like what Anglos called "dirty Mexicans."

Turning, she looked over her shoulder at his mattress. Lifting it all the way up, she saw his hidey hole, a single nail securing a coffee tin's ragged lid. She spun it sideways. Reaching into the hole, she felt around, her fingers touching something furry and stiff. She recoiled, and after catching her breath and telling herself not to be squeamish—she wiped people's asses for a living and if she could deal with excrement, this was nothing—she put her hand in the hole again.

Shredded paper. She pulled it all out, along with a poor dead mouse. The paper made up a punctured sheet that reminded her of the snowflakes from her long-ago days in school. Carefully she smoothed the paper across the mattress. An official document of some kind. State of California. The name of a man she'd heard her father mention. Oliveira. At the bottom of the letter, she saw the man's brown-inked signature. How exactly this Oliveira had cheated her father, she could no longer remember, only that it had to do with why her father had fled California. He'd always told her there was money due, that he had papers to prove it, and she wondered if these had been the papers, the record of his years as a *bracero*. Maybe he'd kept them to show he'd existed, that the State of California had blessed the labor of his hands with its official, brown-bear seal.

She opened a latch beneath the bed to discover a storage space, empty apart from a train lantern whose chimney had not been washed and whose kerosene had hardened into a yellow bolus. Putting the lantern aside, she felt up where the papers had been and discovered the sharp corners of a wooden box. A cigar box. Tugging it, she tried to take it down, but her father had attached it so firmly it wouldn't budge.

#

Fourth grade was the year they began living in La Junta. He had found the boxcar when he'd ridden into town from the ranch, and he had come all the way to Cheraw, where her mother had found a job changing sheets in a hotel, enough to pay for the small adobe building out behind someone's grand, new home. And Salina remembered the cold ride in the back of a pickup truck, her mother holding her belly, and she, with her arms around her little sisters, shrunk down to keep the wind from blowing her hair. By the time they reached town it had been hours since they'd had a drink of water. Her mother had looked around the dusty streets and begun crying. "It will be fine," her father had promised. "Don't worry. I have prepared a new home, and it will cost us nothing to live there."

It was a year after they'd settled in that the accident happened.

She remembered only that they hauled water from a red pump at a farm house that had burnt down, and since she was the oldest, she walked with him to carry water. Before the days of plastic, the containers—jerry cans—weighed nearly as much as the liquid they held. She must have been nine or ten, maybe as old as eleven. It was when she still wanted to be with her father, when she desperately wanted to win his smile.

On this particular day, her father sang songs from his youth. It hadn't started snowing, or at least no snow had accumulated on the ground. Droplets of breath froze in her nostrils, and when she asked her father if he could pump the handle while she took a drink, he said yes, and told her to open her mouth. She'd never been sure how her tongue attached itself to the handle. Maybe he'd told her to put it there. For a long time she'd thought so and held it against him, but now she thought she'd made that up, one insult that stood for the many insults of poverty she had absorbed. More likely some boy at school had put her up to it because it was a kid's prank. She only remembers that her father had shouted, "Don't do that!" and pushed her away, leaving her taste-buds and a layer of skin.

The first month her tongue had bled and bled. Pulling off the gauze only made it bleed more, and she sat mute in the back row at school, not daring to speak. Even this many years later, there were still things she couldn't taste. Salt, for instance. Lemons. Parmesan cheese, which she could feel as gritty slivers, but never craved.

#

When he'd pointed down the road at the caboose, the deacon had said he'd swing back by the church in an hour. He had to see a man about a horse. She could stay out at her father's place, if she had a mind to, but the caboose was the last place she wanted to stay. No, she'd be fine at the church.

She shut off the propane—no sense wasting fuel. The caboose grew instantly frigid, and walking back, her burden of clothing heavier with each step, her elongated shadow looked like a ghost's. After going around to the back of the church, she found the key and let herself in. She dropped the clothes by the wardrobe and rubbed her hands.

Father Rodriguez would know who needed these things most. Or she would ask Dr. Clancy if there was a woman with children who might like to cut up the fabric for a rag rug. That is what her mother would have done, cut every bit of fabric into inch-wide strips and sewn them all together.

A lifetime's work went into her mother's rug, which grew wider by the year, and eventually allowed them to step on the boxcar's floor with bare feet. Salina's job was to wind the endless rag-ball, and when she'd finished her homework, her eyes straining in the flickering light of the kerosene lamp, she would pick up the wooden crochet hook and, sitting cross-legged on the floor, hook the rug's circumference, her hands always busy with that work or some other. Half asleep, she would have heard the boxcar's door slide its final inches shut or the poof as her father blew out the light and murmured in Spanish, "Sleep well, children."

There was so much to remember. The dry air. The way it opened her nostrils. The intermittent shush of passing cars. Dr. Clancy had left the door unlocked, and until he returned, she would give herself a moment of quiet reflection. She pushed open the door to the nave, and there her father sat, hands on his knees, dressed in a black, wool suit with wide lapels, white hair slicked back in a ponytail. Hugo Limone. His skin no longer looked young. It had more wrinkles that any old man's she had ever seen, but if that skin had been stretched out, plumped out by nourishment and youth, she would have recognized the man whose blessing she'd not asked for when she left. She remained standing by the altar, afraid that he was a ghost rather than the man who had sent a piece of his heart traveling with her wherever she went. Finally, the pounding in her chest subsided.

He stood and moved out of the pew. He had shrunk since she'd seen him last, or else she had grown.

Callused fingers pressed her cheeks. In the black irises of his eyes flashed tiny, moonlit windows. "*M'hijita.*" My little daughter.

A cry of rage and anguish escaped. Then she fell against his shoulder and allowed herself to be comforted.

Jaki McCarrick

The Emperor of Russia

I could hear my father singing in the lower field. In between the lines of the poorly-sung Joe Dolan number he would call for me, each time more demanding, though he did not bother to draw near to where I actually was, which was at the back of the house, pegging his newly-washed clothes to the line. I knew I'd give in eventually to his calls, but I wanted him to hurt his voice as much as possible with the screeching. 'Rose! Come down to the big tree,' he said, finally, his song ended. When I finished the laundry, I sauntered towards him. Course it was me who let out the loudest screech of all when I got to the lower field, where he stood by the eucalyptus tree in his brown pinstripe suit with its shiny stains and frayed cuffs, leaning on his pellet gun. Hanging from a high branch of the tree was a crow, plump and stiff, and I knew straight away by the white in its feathers that it was Hermione, my brother's pet, and that my bastard father had killed her. I fell to my knees and cried out, worse than any time when he'd left us first and gone to England.

'Crows are a dime a dozen, wee one, and you better stop with that whining,' my father said. There wasn't an ounce of remorse in his voice.

'You'd no business doing that,' I said.

'I told you what we'd be doing to stop the crop getting took off us from under our noses, didn't I? A certain measure your mother would have none of. But she's not here now is she?' He was right, of course: he had told me what he planned to do to a crow, and yes, my mother wasn't around to protest. She'd died in the years he was away, and here he was now, as he'd been this past while, acting as if he knew everything about how to run our farm, when truth was he knew next to nothing about farming. He was just as he was before; all he was good for was guns and shooting and everyone knew it.

Hanging a dead crow from a tree is a practice they used do in the country, in the border areas especially, to ward off other crows from the new barley, wheat, spuds. The belief was that crows, being sensitive, intelligent birds, would spend a week 'waking' their fellow (dead) crow, and in that time the crop would be harvested. I'd seen it once before, years ago, a pair of crows hanging from blue rope off the gate to a backwoods field in Omeath.

'Julian's been rearing her since she was a chick fell out of her nest,' I said. 'The one white wing, the crack in the beak. How could you do a thing like that?' I went to the ladder lying in the grass by my father's feet, picked it up and brought it to the tree.

'What you doing, Rose?' he said, as I rested the ladder against the eucalyptus.

'Going burying this bird that's what. I'll not have it swinging around for you to poke and swing, and for to call me down from the house to goad at.' On the third step of the ladder I winced at the grip of his sizeable fingers.

'You'll not be burying this bird today,' he said. I couldn't help myself then and looked him straight in the eye and said:

'Well, aren't you the bastard Ma married.' He went to slap my face, as he'd done a few times before, though he stopped due to the stern look I gave him. It is hilarious to consider how much respect my father demands from me and Julian. It's like he thinks that by virtue of the fact of having conceived us he's the right to the utmost loyalty and respect. Though from where I stood on the ladder, eye-to-eye with him, I could see I had crossed a line, and what's more it felt bad to cross it, as I too held some weird store in his having conceived me, if even he had done that.

'You kill a crow, it keeps the rest of them off your field, and you know why?' he said.

'No.'

'Because the others will wake him.'

'The bird was a her,' I said.

'Because the others will wake *her*. They'll screech and croak and they'll not eat, just go back to the trees and cry for a day. That's when we harvest. And we'll not be robbed blind by them then. You see? That's how it was done in the old days. It's the crows or us.'

I got off the ladder and paced about on the grass. What was I going to tell Julian? I had so much hope in his recent sense of happiness with Hermione. I was planning to leave home the following May, you see; I'd a job lined up and everything – in a summer camp in New Jersey – so how could I leave Julian here now with our father, who insisted upon running the farm according to rumour and myth rather than sound agricultural knowledge?

'Haven't the crows as much right to the crop?' I said.

'What you know about anything?'

'I know I can't leave our fella here with you the way you are, going round killing innocent animals.'

'I don't care what you do,' my father said, and looked up at the sky, at the slowly circling crows, who must have been appalled at the sight of one their own tied to a eucalyptus tree like some kind of offering or 'strange fruit'. My father was certainly the lynching kind after all, except that this was the Irish border and not Alabama, though bar the weather and accents the two places are twins on many levels.

'They'll start up now with their waking, and in the

morning we'll reap this harvest and we'll have what we reap all to our bloody selves,' he said. I watched him walk off towards the house. When he was out of sight I could hear the front door open, then shut, though I was sure he would watch me from the window in case I'd climb up the tree and cut down the bird: I thought better of doing that.

The following day, a team of men arrived from Bush to help with the harvest. I'd seen some of them before, in town, or in church; Poles and Lithuanians who'd been hired by neighbouring farms for the potato picking. In the yard, where they'd parked their cars, I met them with my father and shook the burly pickers' hands as he'd instructed me to do. I gave them a few lines about seeing some of them in town and how I'd love to travel to their beautiful countries, which they must be missing in this hole of a place, etc etc. My father quickly took over then and told them about Hermione. As he stood chattering amongst them, I slipped away and went to the house. I'd not had a chance to talk to Julian about her – not alone at least (my Da had watched me like a hawk the night before) and I was waiting for my opportunity.

I threw stones at Julian's window, which was open a little. The thick lace curtains inside moved gently in the breeze. Julian didn't answer, and I didn't want to go inside for fear of my father catching me talking to him and squealing about the bird. He never likes me talking to Julian. He especially doesn't like squealing; has some weird 'code' about it. So I decided that with my father holding court with the pickers, like a big bear or some clownish figure from a Shakespearian play, that I'd talk to my brother from the safety of the front garden.

'Julian, did you see we're to have a big harvest, even with the terrible summer and the rain and all?' I said, but there was no reply.

'Can you see that the field is almost white entirely with the potato flowers? He's a whole team over from Bush today to gather them this year. Listen, about Hermione. I think she's gone, Julian. That's what crows do, Love,' I said. I wanted to tell him about my plan, but thought better of shouting it out in case I'd be heard by the pickers or my father. Julian would have understood though, because he knows the whole history of our farm, which is in the district of Grange, in the Cooley Hills, County Louth. This land is old, with dozens of brown information signs to do with the legends of the Táin, the oldest legend in Europe, about Cú Chulainn and Queen Maebh, dotted about the place. There are wells and souterrains all over, too, old traps and holes like the ones that'd be in Alice in Wonderland. Only they're not Wonderland. They're dark and cold inside, sometimes lined with stone but more often than not it's just the bog down there, which is much worse, as it's darker and weirder than stone when all around you. And if you were ever to get *stuck* down one of those traps or holes you'd never again get out, especially if someone were to block the entrance. The bad thing about our beautiful fields, of course, is that they *are* so lovely, full of clover and all manner of flowers, the harebells in May, the foxgloves in June, so that you'd never know they are also full of such dangers, such *holes*. And a person, a man for instance, who'd been away, who'd fecked off, left his wife and children fending for themselves in these hinterland fields with all their hidden dangers, might not be so *used* to them holes and wells and tunnels and traps, and one day when he's ... But I digress. I did not discuss my plan with Julian, nor had I the heart to tell him the truth about Hermione. Julian was housebound, and unless he stuck his head out his window he'd never see the crow hanging from the eucalyptus tree, so I hoped he would believe me that Hermione had flown away. My father called out. 'What you want now?' I said.

'We're starting. Lads are ready. Not a living crow in sight neither. All cleared off into the hazel wood. Stop slacking now, Rose.' I felt the usual rage at him rise up in me. I wondered why it was he bothered me so much. He should not have had such a hold over me (I hardly knew him after all), but he had. I returned to the window:

'Julian? I'm serious. I need you to get well and strong and not leave me to that stranger we've let back in the house. Treats me like his slave. Like Ma.' And as I said those words I thought I could hear Julian crying and I began to feel ashamed.

'Ah sure, I know you loved him. Wasn't he a funny old Da when we were tiny? Swinging us round the place. But he's not the same. He's not. And I need you to get strong, Julian, so we can take steps. Because that's what we need to do.'

*

He doesn't know this, my father, whose name is Dan, but I keep a photo of him when he was in his teens, maybe my age now. I keep it under my pillow. He would be very surprised to find it there, that's for sure. It's black and white and as old as Methuselah. In the photo he's holding a greyhound puppy, and there's a smile across his face as wide as a sea. One that exudes gushing unadulterated joy. His eyes water with it. His love for the puppy is all over that photograph, like a good sort of stain. Yet whenever I asked him about having a pup or dog as a boy, he would shrug and say he'd never any time for animals when he was young, that he'd never any pets. So, I believe something happened him after he joined the Republican 'war', as he calls it, which he joined when he was fifteen. He not only put away childish things, as they say, but he put away the child, and any memory of him. There is something about the photo that helps me exist in the same house as my father, that makes me think he is not a monster. Even though there are others in the vicinity of the border who think differently.

*

'You're taking long enough with that grub, Rose,' my father said, like the greatest nag that ever lived. I'd made the sandwiches earlier that morning. And I'd been *very* careful and precise about making them, measured you might say, though I lied to buy time at the window with my brother.

'I've to make it yet,' I said.

'Well hurry up about it. Come on.'

'Coming Da. Coming.'

When I got back to him with the grub, I invited my father to eat with me, away from the pickers, who were gathered now round a long table we'd set out in the yard-cum-car-park. He liked seeing I'd taken care with his lunch and that I'd packed it in a picnic basket along with a check tablecloth. He always likes to be treated nicely, my father, delicately even, like bone bloody china, such is the man's vanity. I guided him to sit at the edge of the field, where the land is flat. I laid out the cloth and placed the sandwiches and flask and teacups on it. He tucked in immediately. 'That's a fine lunch you packed us, Rose. You not having any?' he said.

'No.'

'You'll make some fella a fine wife one day,' he said. Did he not see I was far from being interested in men, having had him as a father and therefore a good reason to hate the entire male species?

'La-la-la-la-la …' I said.

'What you la-laing at?' he said, and stuffed a hunk of bread into his mouth.

'Making me sick with that kind of talk, Da,' I said, and sipped on my Diet Coke, watching out of one eye in case any of the pickers came upon us.

'Only I suppose he'd have to cut your tongue out in order to get through a day in peace,' he said, and threw back his head and laughed. My father's jokes are always laced with cruelty, but, annoyingly, they are also told well, and with expert timing.

'Lovely thing to say to me, Da,' I said, and sat back on the grass, my feet on the cloth. I looked at him directly and nearly blurted out there and then exactly what I'd put in the sandwiches.

'Well, it's true,' he said. 'You've repelled every fella came gathering spuds and barley here this past two years.'

'Me and fellas is not your concern,' I said. There was a period of silence between us then and I felt myself dying to tell him what I'd done but stopped myself in time. 'So, you like my sandwiches do you?' I said. He grunted something and nodded. Seeing as he couldn't speak with the relish leaking out of his gob, I decided to make it even more difficult for him. 'Which one do you like most?'

'Most, I like the beef,' he said, and licked his lips.

'Ah, the beef,' I said. 'Well the beef I knew you'd go for. The beef I knew you'd like. So they're the ones I paid most attention to.' I watched him as he sucked carefully each of his fat fingers, probably thinking the only reason I was put on this earth was to serve him, like he was some sort of king or emperor. He'd been the same way with my mother.

'Well, you're a good cook anyways. That's something,' he said. He swallowed the food, wiped his mouth with his sleeve and made an almighty burp. Then he began to snigger. 'I suppose if the fella was deaf you'd be all right,' he said. 'Deaf, and fucken half-blind maybe.' And he rolled about laughing, slapping the tablecloth rapidly as if he'd said the funniest thing.

'Ah that's it, you go right ahead. Entertain yourself with your own jokes,' I said. 'I'd say you're very good at that now, entertaining yourself. Seeing as you were gone out of this house almost twelve years roaming the streets of places, sure you must be a grandmaster of entertaining yourself by now.' He knew where I was going with this, where I always went: berating him for leaving us, all those years before. He lit up a cigarette without offering one to me.

'I came home not to see you reared without a mother. Because I care. Because I'm your father. And what went on between her and me is not *your* concern neither,' he said, sniffily. He stood and looked towards the pickers, who were already back at their work in the fields. We could hear their voices coming close, their fractured laughter floating on the air. 'You ask them lads to go from the drills that side?' he said, perplexed.

'I did,' I replied. 'That's how we've done it all these years. Left to right.'

'Good to split the work up I suppose,' he said.

'I thought we'd start this end now you're finished eating,' I said, and showed him the sacks I'd brought for the spuds we were yet to pick.

'Just this is the rough side, rolls down to ditches and all, and I would have thought you'd have preferred, you know, an easier go of it,' he said. I shook my head.

'If you start left we'll meet the lads coming halfway, you see? I'll go right,' I said. We stood and put the picnic things away. We folded up the tablecloth, corner to corner, and I was surprised he remembered how to do it. As we met with the folding of the cloth, I felt a pang of guilt in my heart and tried to shake it off. He saw it of course, the confused flicker of love in my eyes.

'I thought of you all the time wee one. When I was away. You and Julian. You been talking to him?' I nodded and felt the burn of his eyes on me.

'What does he say now?'

'Not much. He wants to forget about it. The accident. Who wouldn't want to forget a thing like that, nearly took your life, made you a ghost of your former self,' I said. My father nodded and looked out at the land. Before us was Carlingford Lough, blue and flat. I would miss the sight of the Lough in America. The day was bright, the heather on the hills turning a soft aubergine colour. My father seemed fixed on the road towards Carlingford.

'Down there,' he said, 'the road North. I remember it well. Men in uniform. "Papers, Paddy" – and me not yards from my own farm.'

'I've no memory of those days and I don't want to have either,' I said.

'Well I do,' he said, and I felt a little ashamed for offering him no understanding on this subject.

'Why d'you go to England then if you hate it so much?' I said.

'We all run back to the colonizer, to the one that hurts us – eventually. Do you not know that, Rose? Didn't your mother teach you how that game worked? They take something from you, a part of your heritage, your identity, that you *need* so as to know yourself, and you go always looking for that thing.' I knew there was something in what my father said. To do with our history here, perhaps. About how the border area, all three hundred twisty-turny miles of it, had been ravaged by the Troubles. How it had formerly been plagued by checkpoints and police and soldiers. My father knew things. And if I could have removed the bitterness I felt towards him from my heart I might have learned some of them. There was a moment then between us; in fact it was the culmination of many moments, when I felt he was the grand figure, the giant I'd made him into when I was a child. He felt awkward then, I could see it in him, though he quickly lapsed, purposefully it seemed to me, into the crow-killing coward I'd become more used to, as if this were a mask, one behind which he felt safe: 'Well, the spuds won't be lifted by themselves,' he said, rubbing his hands together. 'And we better get into it before the crows stop caring.'

As he picked along his drill, I slipped away from him and went back to the house. The window was again open in Julian's room at the front and I threw stones against the pane for my brother to show himself, but as was his way he did not come. I directed my voice to the window: 'Julian. You remember when he was gun-running? Hiding guns all over Ma's land? Putting us all in danger? Well, he was a bad egg then and he's bad egg now. So you better hang in there, and stop moaning, sounding so lost and sad.' I said. 'Hermione's a fucken stupid name for a crow anyways. As if I didn't know where you got it. Look, buck up. Because we're to be free soon, the two of us, of the stranger we let back in this house when we shouldn't have.' I sensed Julian would know what I meant and what I was planning now to do.

When I got back to the meadow I saw my father

retching over the white potato flowers. I'd brought another sack with me, flung over my shoulder. I went to him and asked him to lean on me so I could bring him back to the house. 'Into the meadow here, by the crocus. That's it, Da,' I said. I took a few paces with him and stopped. 'Rest here on this big stone a while. Sit, and I'll see if I can find you some wild mint that'll settle your stomach and then we'll go home,' I said. As he sat on the stone, clinging to his stomach, I rummaged around in the grass, not for mint at all, as you can imagine. Eventually, I found what I was looking for. My father whined with pain and I did my best not to pay any heed.

'Oh Rose, I've something to tell you, love,' he said, as he wiped down his sweaty brow.

'Too late for talk like that, Da,' I said. 'I'd save it for Julian. He's the young one now.'

'Isn't it *about* Julian,' my father said. He looked about him, his wide eyes darting from rock to bush. 'This bit of your mother's land. Ah, we would walk here many's a time. Looks very familiar. During my "political career" perhaps. Aye, I'm sure this is a place I've been to and hidden certain things in.'

'Much good your politics did you. Much good it did any of us. Had to go to England in the end, left us half-starved most of the time.' I stood him up and walked him towards where I'd rummaged. He sort of half-hummed, half-sang as he walked: '*Oh me oh my, oh me oh my, you're such a good-looking woman.*' I pressed on his shoulder and urged him to stop.

'Now where's that mint?' He said. And with that I pushed him into the hole that had been hidden all these years in the grass. He let out a roar as he fell. I knew all about the holes and souterrains on this land, as I'd farmed it for years without my father's help. As he cried, I pulled Hermione from the sack I'd brought with me, and threw her down on top of him.

'There,' I said to the mouth of the hole, 'the crows can mourn the two of yez now. Because I won't, nor will Julian. "Crow's wake!" This is modern Ireland and we don't string up crows no more! And if anyone comes looking for you, Da, I'll say he fecked off to England as he was wont to do. And I'll be believed. I'm a young woman with prospects, off to America for a job that's lined up already, a brother, half-dead from a joy-riding accident, and a feckless father who has nothing to do now there's peace in Ireland only to tell me how to work my own farm. No one will come looking for you here, Da, because no one will fucken miss you.'

'Rose, Rose!' my father screamed. I went to the stone and began to roll it towards the mouth of the hole. It was tough going as over and over I rolled it.

'I'll be rolling the stone over now, Da, so you'll have to shut up,' I said.

'Rose, Rose!' he continued. What did he want to say? That he was sorry for the life he'd made us all lead? The hard work and the poverty, that had undoubtedly caused my mother's early death? It was too late for apologies.

'What is it, Da? I can't let you out. You go stringing things up that people love; you go slapping me and me eighteen years old. You're no good. And no good for Julian, who is my only friend here at all.' And then he said the words that deep down I knew were true:

'Rose, Julian's dead this two years.'

'What are you talking about, you mad bastard?'

'After the accident, sure you went demented. What with your mother and all.'

'What's that?'

'You started talking to him six months later. And I always thought that somewhere in your mind you must have known Julian wasn't in that room.' I cried out then. My hands shook and I retched into the grass though I'd eaten nothing.

'What about Hermione?'

'Who?'

'The crow! The crow down there on top of you. Who reared it from a chick if it wasn't Julian?'

'He did. But that was long ago. If this is that bird, it's come back after a long time away, just like myself. Julian's dead, daughter, and you better believe it. So, you go rolling that stone over this hole you'll have no one at all. No Ma, no brother, no Herm…'

'Hermione.'

'And no Da! You'll be an orphan entirely.' I knew then he was right. Wasn't he always? Though I wished he'd said something about Julian before. I was embarrassed to think he knew all along I'd been talking to a ghost.

'Oh Da,' I cried, 'why'd you have to kill that crow?'

'I'm sorry about it. Oh me stomach.'

'That'll be the strychnine,' I said.

'The what?'

'I poisoned the beef.'

'Oh Rose. Why d'you have to do a thing like that?'

'You shouldn't have gone away, Da. That's when, when it all started.'

'What Rose, what?'

'Oh, didn't I miss you, Da?' I said, and felt something inside me begin to shatter. What had I done? Bad enough I'd poisoned my own father, but now he was at the bottom of a cold deep pit. I thought about screaming out to the pickers for help. I heard him laughing. I drew closer to the edge. There was the sound of a chest or trunk of some kind being opened, of creaking, rusty hinges, and of the clatter of metal within.

'What is it, Da, what's down there?' I said. I could hear him talking away to himself.

'They don't make them like this anymore. Look at the spin on that.'

He shouted my name up at me, his voice full of sorrow and sincerity, like the old Da, the one I'd idolized before he left:

'The bird, Rose. I'm awfully sorry about him,' he said.

'Her Da, her.'

'Where'd our fella get that name anyways?'

'He was studying Shakespeare at school. And I was helping him. *A Winter's Tale* he took that name from,' I said, as tears streamed down my face, the memories of our once vaguely-happy family flooding my mind.

'Right,' my father said.

'"The Emperor of Russia was my father."'

'What's that, Love?' he said.

'You mustn't call me that, Da.' I said. 'You're a stranger to me now.' His voice got quiet then, like a whisper, thin as a goose feather, and I concentrated intently as if it was the last time I might ever hear the tenderness in my father's voice, which had always been there, I realised, had I bothered to listen for it.

'Come here to me, Rose. Come to the edge and I'll see your face just one more time before you roll over that stone, and say again to me the sweet-sounding thing I just heard you say.' So I did. Who could resist the way my charming father could ask a thing? I went close to the hole, my face hanging over its dark mouth, and whispered:

'"The Emperor of Russia was my father."' It was a line from *A Winter's Tale* that I'd always loved. And I meant every soft-sounding syllable.

'I know, Rose. I know,' he said, and swiftly he lifted up the long contraption in his hand, and pointed the dark metal end straight at me. His hands shook. Our eyes, which were similar, round and slate-grey, locked for a second, his betrayal of me and mine of him suspended momentarily outside our eye contact, allowing for this rare exchange of pure familial love, before he fired with his trademark expertise.

Gerard McKeown

Rabbit Season

The first time I held a gun I knew I could never kill with it. Not just humans, animals too. Unlike Emmett, who every Monday would come into school with a new story about killing foxes or badgers on his family's farm. One time he brought in rabbit pie for his lunch – raised on the farm, shot on the farm, baked on the farm – that's how he put it. The girls said he was cruel shooting wee bunnies. Emmett said the wee bastards weren't cute; they bred like mad and ate crops like they were free. If it had been a vicious old fox no one would have given a fuck, except who'd want to eat a fox? Besides, if he hadn't baked the pie, he'd only have dumped the carcass. Jane was one of the girls who called him cruel. I told her he only talked like that to wind them up, but she insisted she hated him; Jane loved animals. She claimed she loved them more than people. She also claimed she was vegetarian, but I caught her at a house party, not long before we broke up, alone in the corner of the kitchen, drunk and stuffing her face with a packet of sliced ham. There was a time that would have been funny.

That Saturday we tucked into one of Emmett's rabbit pies while waiting for the rain to stop. We were over at his granda's farm. His granda had died a year before and left the place to Emmett's dad. The family's proper house was the other side of Rasharkin, but most of the time Emmett stayed here, and most of the time he was by himself.

He cleaned the shotgun at the kitchen table, saying he wished we were hunting rabbits. They were well easy to shoot, bouncing around thinking they were super cute. They learned the truth when he put a round in them. The big hunt was serious business, he claimed; not everyone makes it back alive. I thought he was trying to sound upbeat. That he was embarrassed by what he'd told me a few days before.

We were lucky with the weather in the end. Thick gobs of rain had splattered onto Emmett's windshield the whole drive up the duel carriageway. Emmett had insisted it would stop at noon. It did too, almost to the minute.

'How do you know stuff like that?' I said, wondering if he'd some folksy wisdom that us town folk never bothered with.

'The forecast was on in the car,' he said, with a shrug. 'I just listened to it.'

I'd suggested hanging out in town, smoking a few joints at the old abattoir, but Emmett had packed all that in, in an effort to win back his ex, Anna. He was determined if nothing else. I think really he knew it wasn't going to happen, but he needed time, and activities to take his mind off her. That's why we were out shooting today.

Emmett said it was important I got a feel for the gun, so I wouldn't be scared of it. He made me carry it all the way from the farmhouse. When he handed it to me, I thought of Wee Dan's BB gun in school, until then, the closest I'd come to holding a real gun, but that was a toy; you'd have needed to fire it at point-blank range to do any damage. This shotgun was made to destroy things. Emmett had killed with it.

On our way to the field Emmett explained that the gun had two triggers, one for each barrel. We'd take turns shooting, two rounds each. I caught a glimpse of a rabbit bouncing in under a blackberry bush. It didn't bother me that I'd just eaten its cousin, its brother, or even its mother, but I didn't tell Emmett about it in case he wanted to shoot it. I remembered that scene in *A Very Long Engagement* where the farmer says war took all the killing out of him. That he had to get his wife to kill the rabbits. That was one of the few scenes where I'd stayed awake, and although Jane wasn't pleased with me, she was more forgiving in those days.

'You ready?' Emmett shouted from across the field. I held the gun ready and gave him a thumbs up. The clay pigeon shot up out of the trap, spinning across the sky like a flying saucer. I couldn't believe I was about to fire a gun. That with one crook of my finger a spray of pellets would tear the clay apart. As the clay started to lose height, I remembered I was supposed to be tracking it. There was no time to take aim. I swung the barrel round hoping for the best. The shot roared in my ear before I felt it. The kick, which Emmett had warned me about, slammed the butt hard against my shoulder.

'Fuck,' I shouted. The heavy butt fell quickest, striking the ground with a crack. My eyes followed the sound, locking with the nostrils of the gun, as it stood upright, pointing into my face, threatening to blow its last round through me. I dived out of the way, too late if it had mattered, flinging the shotgun from me like a rounders bat. Lying flat on the grass, as the morning's rain soaked into my clothes, I thought I'd shat myself. Emmett's laugh boomed out as he came running across the field. I scrambled onto my feet again, glad nothing ran down my leg. Thank fuck. I grabbed the gun up off the grass. Whatever went round school on Monday, I didn't want him saying I was scared of it. It had taken all my balls to lift it.

'I warned you,' he said. 'It's got some kick to it.'

I hated the wide open laugh plastered across his face. Some nasty words slid to the front of my mouth, but I swallowed them.

'That nearly fired at me,' I said.

'That only happens in films. To fire this, you have

to pull the trigger, one of them anyway. Do you want to go again?'

I shook my head.

'Go on. Don't be afraid. You'll probably have a bruise tomorrow. You'd like to think you hit something for your trouble.'

He ran back laughing to the trap, detouring to pick up my undamaged clay. I would hit it this time, just to salvage a bit of pride when he told the story at school. Only earlier I'd thought it was good to see him cheered up, even if I knew he was pretending. Now he was genuinely happy I wanted him to go back to walking around like a half-shut knife, crying about Anna, who'd made a dick out of him behind his back.

He shouted across the field to see if I was ready. I bounced the gun lightly in my grip. So it wouldn't have fired when I dropped it? Despite knowing this, my body still shook. In that split second when I was peering down the barrel, I really thought I was about to die. Funny, that instead of anything profound coming to mind, I reckoned the barrel would taste metallic. That would have been my last thought. It wasn't even original. At school Emmett had told me he put both barrels in his mouth last weekend – cartridges loaded and a head full of Anna. He thought he was a coward because he couldn't pull the trigger. I didn't know if it was bravado, or if I should tell someone. I chickened out. That's why I agreed to shoot clays; I felt guilty. I wondered why he told me, of all people, maybe because I'd been dumped the month before him. I was handling it better though. Despite thinking of Jane every day, and the fact that, if she wanted, I'd get back with her in a second, the worst I'd done was punch a wall.

I gave Emmett a wave and closed my right eye, lining the nub at the end of the barrel up between the two sights. I wondered if I could have hit him at this distance. I was careful not to look like I was aiming for him. He'd have taken the gun off me and made me walk the whole ten miles back to town.

As Emmett released the trap I tracked the clay, again watching it almost too long. It started to fall slowly; the air cushioning its hollow bottom, as it completed its arc. Tightening my finger over the second trigger, I felt the blast of the shotgun, felt it struggle to kick gripped tight against my shoulder. I held it steady and watched the clay pigeon shatter in the air.

'Cracker fucking shot,' Emmett shouted. 'Want another go?'

I grinned, though my shoulder stung like fuck.

He came running over with the box of cartridges, flipped open the barrel and put the empty shells in his pocket. He loaded two more and handed the gun back to me.

'Thanks for coming out here,' he said. 'You know, weekends have been the hardest. What with you lot all being in town, and me out here on my puff.'

I looked down at the barrel briefly, then back up at him and smiled. It was a practiced smile, that allowed me to end conversations without speaking. Emmett kept looking at me, as if he wanted more. I wanted to look away, self-conscious of what Emmett could read. I waited for him to turn back to the trap. When he finally ran across the field, I raised the gun and aimed at him. I knew if I fired, I would kill him. I tried to imagine that rush of power I'd read about in accounts of people on rampages, tried to imagine it was close by, close enough for me to pretend I felt it.

I'd shot Emmett before, when Wee Dan brought his BB gun into school back in first year, trying to convince people he was in some youth wing of a paramilitary group. We all took turns messing about with it in the locker bays, pinging it off the metal doors. Received wisdom says not to point guns at people; an old saying of my dad's, who grew up on a farm himself, was 'never fire an empty gun at someone; fate might put a bullet in the chamber.' And sure, hadn't I fired every pellet out of that little bastard before I pointed it at the back of Emmett's head. I'd even fired it a few extra times to make double sure it was empty. When he turned around, I fired straight into his eye. What a laugh it would have been to see him shit himself. As I heard the cheap plastic crack of the trigger, I saw a little yellow ball come whizzing out. Only Emmett's reaction of jerking his head back made the ball ping off his cheek instead. He fell to the ground screaming. The crowd around us were caught between going to his aid or swinging their fists at me, but I'd seen it up close; his eye was safe, and that was all that mattered. He'd a nasty bruise for the next week, while I was off suspended. Wasn't I doing something just as stupid now?

I lowered the gun before he reached the trap, and watched him load another clay, oblivious to what had been going on behind his back. I hit the clay a cracker, and the next. I couldn't believe how easily I'd got the hang of shooting.

'My go,' Emmett shouted, running back across the field. 'You're on the trap.'

When I handed him the gun he froze, and pulled a face, as if he'd remembered he'd left the oven on.

'How you holding up since you got dumped?' he asked.

'Fine,' I said, looking round.

'Think you'll ever get her back?'

'Jane? Naw. That girl can suck shite through a

beehive.'

'Wish I felt like that,' he said, nodding at the gun.

'Takes time,' I said.

'You've probably the next one lined up, knowing you.'

I laughed, still not looking at him. 'Yeah right. Think I'll keep clear of girls for a bit.'

He snapped the barrel shut. I flinched. He saw it too. A funny look passed between us that seemed to confirm I'd reason to flinch. His face was blank, as if trying to give nothing away, but an intensity brewed on it. I thought to grab the gun.

He stepped back, far enough so he could swing the gun round for a shot. I wondered if I should speak. Tell him it was just one night. That she came on to me, and you know what Anna's like; she's had everything between her legs but a bar of soap. I wasn't the first either. She'd been round half our group, some of them before she dumped him. And sure, hadn't I lost enough, losing Jane. The rest of those fuckers got off scot-free.

'You know, I still have nightmares about that time I shot you,' I said. 'Where you don't move in time and I take your eye out.'

'Why you bringing that up?'

'Just a thought. Something I've never told anyone.'

'You're loading the trap,' he said, motioning to it with the gun. He looked ready to cry. I opened my mouth but could think of nothing else to say. I could have dived at him, but he was ready to turn both barrels on me if I tried.

I turned my back and set off across the field. I'd heard somewhere that if you're being shot at you should run in a zig-zag. Doubt that would work at close range, not against a spray of pellets and a good shot. The stone walls were close, and they'd shield me, but I'd never reach them, no matter how hard I sprinted; they might as well have been at infinity. Reaching the trap seemed equally unlikely, but I estimated the number of steps and started counting down, wondering if I'd reach zero. Even the thought of the sound of the gun gave me goose bumps. I wondered if that was the last time I'd feel my flesh prickle. But weren't pellets faster than sound. Wouldn't I feel them slice through me before I heard them? I looked down expecting to see my guts burst out of my stomach as those tiny metal balls lacerated me. Maybe that was only in movies too. Maybe it would feel like the time I smoked too much dope and every breath tickled, as if bubbles were rising through my chest. Would I go into shock? Would I be dead before the sound of the shot reached me?

But I did hear the gun. The first shot made me freeze. With the second one I almost screamed. I turned mid-field to see Emmett standing there stunned. Even at this distance I could see he was shaking. I ran towards him, hoping I'd reach him before he could reload.

'It was a rabbit,' he stammered, looking like a child who'd broken the best ornament in the house. His hand shook as he passed me the gun, but the second I had it, he seemed to recover.

'It looks like rain,' he said. 'Let's not shoot anymore.'

'Shouldn't we cover the trap?' I said, attempting to act normal. My voice had a hoarseness to it.

'It's a rusty piece of shit,' he said. 'We're getting a new one next month anyway.'

The whole way to the house, I held on tight to the gun. Neither of us spoke.

When we got back, Emmett's car wouldn't start. I didn't believe him, but I was glad to get away from him, even if I had to walk home. Emmett kept apologising, but in a half-hearted way. I was only too happy to put as much distance between us as I could. As I said goodbye, he gave me the strangest look, one I'd never seen on another person, a shocked weariness, like he was watching a ghost that didn't know it was dead.

I couldn't stop thinking about that look the whole walk back. After a third car passed me on that quiet road, I was too spooked to follow the directions he'd given me. I cut across the fields to a river I knew would lead me back to town. It was night before I reached home. When I got in, I stood for a long time looking at myself in the mirror, not thinking how I looked, only that I was there.

Jay Merill

Vole or Mole

It's a golden-shiny day and I'd like to get a lolly. I look into Blakemore's shop but I'm not going in if Mrs Sturridge is there. Because when I went in last week to buy an ice-cream she said 'Give me a break,' just because I asked her what was the difference between the fudge flavoured and the toffee flavoured. But she isn't, so I go inside. I choose a purple lolly. Blackcurrant.

My mother does not like blackcurrant so we never have blackcurrant jam at home, we only ever have raspberry or strawberry. My mother said blackcurrant was the only jam her mother ever made and she remembered when she was ill in bed once with scarlet fever that her mother kept on bringing in platefuls of toast spread thick with blackcurrant jam. She said the very sight made her sick. I'm not sure if she meant it gave her a fed-up feeling or it made her really sick. I can't help getting a picture of real slimy sick sogging into the bedcovers. But if I ask her again she'll just shrug the thought away hurriedly and won't bother to answer me. So I'll never know. She always does that if I try to go over something to get clear about what actually happened. I looked up *sick* in the dictionary and came across the word *vomit*. It was new to me and I liked the look of it so I've added it to my list of words to use.

I lick the lolly very carefully to try and find out what is so bad about the blackcurrant flavour. There is something dense about it that lies underneath the sweet taste. I get that. But anyway, is the blackcurrant lolly the same as blackcurrant jam? I try to work out if a strawberry lolly tastes like strawberry jam, and I think it does, a little bit. It's hard to see them as connected though because one is cold and the other is warmish. The lolly is made of ice and if you don't eat it fairly quickly it could melt away to nothing. It is so hot today that I can feel the lolly turning watery straight away. Drips are running down through my fingers. I suck it quickly and notice the colour turn to mauve. When I look in the mirror in the window of Tyne's boutique on Green Street I notice my mouth has purple stains at the corners. Sticking out my tongue I find that is purplish too. Oh well! I carry on to the corner and cross the zebra crossing. And there, on the other side of the pavement, is Brian Barlow, the boy who cannot speak.

Usually Brian is busy chugging along by the kerb, being a train or a bus. But today he is just standing still with his hands held together in front of his face. He looks as if he's saying a prayer. A prayer is made up of words though, isn't it? Which makes me wonder if he knows about words. Even though he's not able to say them out loud. Or, can you say a prayer without words coming into it? Like you can picture a dish of strawberries and know you want to eat them without words making the wish. And you can know the strawberries in the dish will not be like the strawberry of strawberry jam or the taste of a strawberry lolly without having to say the smallest thing. Which proves words are not everything. I'm going to the Old Farm to see if any of my friends are there. It's where we usually hang out.

Then an amazing thing happens. Brian Barlow smiles at me. I have never seen him smile before except at his make-believe passengers. His smile is wide and happy but it makes me feel uneasy. I am frightened of something. But I don't know of what. And I edge closer in slowly, not wanting to go right up to him but wanting to see what he is doing with his hands. Has he learnt to play 'Here's the Church and Here's the Steeple...' where you have to hold your two hands upright with your fingertips pressed together pretending they are a steep church roof? After this you tuck your fingers in so they can't be seen, but have to keep the indexes pointing upwards leaning against one another. They are the steeple. Then you turn your hands palm up... 'And there's the people.' is what you say last of all. You waggle your fingers to show that they are the people and that they're live human beings. Could Brian have learnt that game without knowing what the words were? If so, what would it all have meant to him? No, words are not everything, I see that. But in this game they are telling you the shapes are standing in for a roof and a steeple and then people. My lolly is melting away and trickles have started running down my arm. I eat up what is left of it quickly and throw the stick into the gutter. Anyway, now I'm close by I see that Brian has something in his hands and this is why he is holding them together in that funny way. That's all.

When I get up very close: There's a soft looking moving something. Mouselike, but not quite a mouse. Maybe a vole or a mole. The vole or mole shifts round in Brian Barlow's curved hands. It seems to sniff at his fingers, as though seeking a way out. Why doesn't it jump? Perhaps it's too scared. It won't know where it is, or who or what Brian Barlow is. Will it? The vole or mole has lost its way and now has been caught in a trap. Brian's hands are like a trap because every time the creature sniffs he brings his hands further together, blocking its escape route. Also, I try to count how many vole or mole bodies, (lying flat because they walk on all fours), you would get between the pavement and Brian Barlow's hands. It's hard to work this out but there must be more than a hundred vole or mole body spaces. If there were a hundred of *my* body spaces (upright because I walk on two feet), between me and the ground it would be much too far for me to jump and I would be afraid just the same.

Now the animal is looking upwards at the golden-shiny sun. I see its little pinkish snout as its head lifts up higher and higher. The strips of dark fur poking out through Brian's fingers are tinged with this sun gold. Fear darts through me. I quiver. What will happen? Brian Barlow stands without moving, not being a bus or a train at this moment. Maybe, just being himself? He stares around with this wide fixed smile on his face. And he even seems to see me standing next to him.

Behind the houses of the street where we are standing is a wild field called The Old Farm. Though it isn't farmlike as there's no sign of any such thing as a haystack or a barn. There are pathways here and there and thin bent over trees and three raggedy ponds which are dried out in the summer. But this is where I want to be. There are fronds and grasses and weedy bits. I like coming here and so do most of my friends. The vole or mole cannot escape but I can and do. I jump back and then walk on quickly to the field. But none of the kids I know are there today. And I sit near one of the ponds of old cracked mud and try to think about what to do. I can't seem to put things into words. But I do *know* what I am going to do in any case. I think I already knew before I walked away from Brian Barlow. So I get up and go back. As soon as I reach Green Street again I see that he is standing exactly where he was, with his hands still raised as if they are praying, or playing at being a church. But his back is towards me and I don't know if he's kept up the smile. I go up to him at once as I know I must not stop and consider or I won't do what I am going to do. I still can't put into words what this is but my legs and feet carry me right on up to him all the same.

'Brian, let me see what you've got in your hands,' I call out. I know he can't say any words but this isn't the same thing as not understanding any words. Is it? When he turns round and faces me his great big smile is there as before.

I manage to walk right up to Brian, even though I'm scared of him and of what I'm about to do. Because, what will happen? He opens his hands slightly and I see the small furry animal up close. I ask Brian if I can hold it for just a minute but he keeps on with the smile and does nothing else. So I put out my hands, curved like his and edge them right up to him till I am leaning against the skin of his thumbs. And then I stare into his face. He opens his hands a little more and yes, I think I can just about do it. I dip in and grab the creature; close my hands together. Run. And keep on running. When I get past the lamppost I turn back; see Brian Barlow. His smile is gone. His mouth is open. There's a round horror about the shape of it. His eyes are full of horror too. He is staring. Not at me but up into the sky. His hands are still prayer shaped and held almost level with his head.

I rush to the Old Farm quickly and find a warm soft grassy spot for the animal in my hands. Then I kneel down and let it go. It scoots quickly into the undergrowth. If it's a vole it will find a nice twisty clump to make a home in. If it's a mole it will burrow underground. I know that much. When I get back to Green Street Brian Barlow is still exactly where he was. Just like a statue he does not move.

#

So what did I save? Vole or mole? I can't answer that as I don't know. But the important thing is I did save something. So maybe I don't need to keep the question mark. For sure, when I get home I can check in the encyclopaedia. That'll most likely tell me which it was. Ok, so then there'll be another entry on my list of things I know. There's one matter the encyclopaedia won't help me to sort out though, however many times I ask. Because the answer to one question may not lead to the answer to another. That's why there are always so many of them.

The question I'm talking about is, should I have snatched the animal from Brian Barlow's hands? It was rescuing but it was also stealing. And loads more misty questions are lining up like ghosts behind this one. Like: Was rescuing the creature a good thing? Brian Barlow might have loved it and made a cute little Beatrix Potter type cottage for it in his back garden. In the wild it might get attacked by another creature and die. But, also, Brian Barlow might have killed the creature by accident or because he wanted to see what it felt like to do that. Like when I squished an ant once. And in the wild it might have met a vole or mole friend to set up a nest with. And the Universe! When I say that word I look up at the sky, like the vole or mole did and like Brian Barlow is doing now. What would the Universe want? What?

I stand staring upwards for a few minutes more then carry on home. I see Mrs Sturridge as I go along the street to my house so I look away. She is not my favourite person because my mother said she said, 'There's a child round here as asks too many questions for her own good.'

Meaning me of course. Who else?

Diana Powell

The Watcher

He watched her every day now. Seeing the roll of her body, the slice of her hand through the water, a rhythmic thrust of her feet. He had never seen a woman swim like that before. He had never seen a woman naked.

The first time he saw her, she was heading out of the bay, towards the open sea, where the ships roamed. A place for grey-armoured giants, not tender pink flesh.

'Stop,' he mouthed, as if she could hear him through the drawn-out length of his spy-glass.

And, yes, she did stop, then swung east towards the far shore, away from him, until she disappeared.

The second time, he thought he was watching a seal. He stood on the cliff-top above the village, looking down at a smooth, black head, bobbing between the waves. They were not unheard of in the channel, though not common, unloved by the fishermen. He waited for the creature to dive, but still it hung there, nosing this way and that. He didn't have his glass with him that day. A seal shouldn't stay up that long, a seal couldn't stay up that long. Finally, the head sunk down, to be followed by the arc of an arm breaking the surface. He knew, then, he was looking at the swimmer. And, when she turned and struck for the island, he knew where she came from.

There was a cove on the neighbouring holm, where the trees straggled down to the tide-line; somewhere he could moor the skiff; easy to focus on both sides of the island. This was where he went each morning, getting up an hour early, before he must go further along the coast to check the nets. His father was pleased by this new industry. This was the hour she swam, sometimes starting from the jetty to the west, sometimes from the beach at the far end. The jetty was his favourite; there was more to wait for, as she came down the path from the castle, then stopped at the wall, her lower body kept hidden from him. But he knew what she doing, with the swift dip of each knee, followed by a curtsey. A tug at the shoulders of her dress, another at the ties of her slip, so that she stood there, revealed... but not quite yet.

Something else for his tongue to lick his lips over – the slow drag of her palm, down, up her arm, then around the breast, one side, then the other, as she applied some secret cream. The kneading of her fingers, circling her nipples, her belly. Then she bent down, beneath the wall, and everything he saw was in his head, until she stepped out onto the slipway, her naked length trembling in his glass.

Next, she would tuck her hair into a plain, dark cap, and with head high, arms swinging, she would stride forward, whatever the weather, whatever the strength of the sea. On, into the water up to her waist, before raising her hands skyward, together, to arch down into the waves. Waiting for her to surface, he matched his breath to hers, his lungs tight, his throat mouthing like a netted mackerel. Where was she? How could she stay so long in the airless dark? And then, always at the moment when his body must break under the gush of his trapped breath, her head would rise, and she would shake it from side to side – the seal, again – her arms following, always the left first, to move in perfect rhythm, the water giving way, to let her pass.

Soon, in the town, there was talk of her. He was not the only one to know of her existence. 'German,' he heard, one day on the quay, the word snarled. The memories of the older generation were long. But no, within days it had changed. 'Further north', one of those Scandinavian countries, where their hair was also the colour of Highbourne sand, the voices as hoarse in their throats as the enemy's. He knew little about such places, except there was snow, ice. Perhaps that was why the cold was nothing to her, the water of an English sea in drab autumn feeling warm to her.

She had come to work for the old lady, the landlord of the 'Sailor' said. 'Cook,' he thought, 'housekeeper'; someone to care for the ageing owner in her tumbled-down mansion. But no, it wasn't that, it was nothing like that at all. She was there to keep intruders off the island; no-one was to go there now; odd, the men said, to have a woman for what should be a man's job; why had she been hired, instead of some laid-off crewman? How could *she* keep anyone away? They knew nothing of the power in her taut muscles, her sinewed frame. But it was said she had a gun, and that she had used it. Shots had been heard, quite different from the booming discharges of the pheasant-shooting days. Each day, like the careless, over-fed gulls circling overhead, someone would drop another morsel amongst the eager crowd; each day, someone would preen at their superior knowledge.

But none of them knew her as he did, he was sure. None of them knew her like *this*.

This was what he liked best; better, even, than the careless stripping, the ritual anointing – the moment she climbed out of the water. He was never sure when it would happen; the timing of it varied, according to the length of her swim. Sometimes, she would do no more than one circuit of the island; sometimes, she would head out of the bay, as he had seen her that first time, before turning for the opposite shore, out of sight.

Whenever this happened, he was afraid he would have to leave, that there was no excuse he could make to his father for so long a delay. But, at last, there she was, coming around the point, towards land.

He would fix his spy-glass firm, then, its aim precise, so that nothing was missed.

That first rise as she stopped swimming, pushed her feet down, to feel the sand, and stood up. The water would fall from her, another layer shed, until it settled around her waist. With each firm step, a little more of her body came into the light. The sweep of her hips, the dark valley widening down, down between the firm, round swell of her buttocks. The length of her thigh, lower, past her knee; or up, as it was, as she rose, until she paused, all of her on dry land, from heel to hair-line; bare.

And then she would turn around, back towards the sea, towards him. She would turn, and pull off her cap, and shake her hair free, run her hands through it, then tossing back her head again. There she was, the front of her now, her hands, her arms, her breasts… her breasts, her thighs, shaking, the shining drops of water flying free.

On fine days, she looked towards the sun, and smiled. Or… was she looking at him? He was far away, and hidden well – he thought. Still, on those days, her eyes met his through the glass. But no, it was no more than chance, a trick of the light, a shudder of the lens.

There was more talk of her now. A name he couldn't grasp, to hold in his mind, on account of its strangeness, its hard sounds hewn from her hard language. It didn't matter, he didn't need it. But the knowledge that she was a swimmer for her country – he liked the sense it made. Now he understood why it was so easy for her, why she could go so far, why the currents and waves were nothing to her.

And the gun was a certainty now.

'I saw her,' the harbour-master said.

'She fired at my boat,' the skipper of the 'Northern Lights' swore.

'Keep away from such like, young lad!' they told him.

'Keep away from her,' his father told him, as if he knew.

'Stay away from the island.'

But he didn't go on the island. None of them did, since this latest owner's arrival, with her strange notions and cranky ways, letting plants and animals run wild, so that they tangled together, no better than an incomer's net. Unearthly shrieks tore through the air of the channel, night and day. Creatures that didn't belong, it was said, like the blowsy shrubs, flaunting their brazen colours across the water, reminding him of the holiday-makers and day-trippers, waving their gay handkerchiefs from the paddle-steamers, as they neared the beach.

Last summer, from the dunes, he had watched these women hiding themselves under parasols, magazines, towels, and sun-glasses, until they disappeared into the beach huts. Watched them flinch across the hot sand, as far as the sea's edge. A puppet's dance followed, as a toe went forward, then back, to a squealing accompaniment; hands flicked up, flicked down, knees knocked together. And when, finally, they were thigh-deep, they would wait and wait, before a careful lowering, to stretch their arms forward for one, two strokes, round and back, their legs spreading in unison, with their startled heads kept high above the water. Like frogs. This was all he had then. It had been enough at the time.

They were nothing like his swimmer. He called her 'his' by now. His to look at – it was all he did. Where was the harm in that? To look, and dream, and… There was no need to be careful, or be afraid. He never went on the island, or anywhere close, because 'close' had its dangers, too. Something else that was said in the village – she had capsized one of the boats drifting too near the jetty. So he kept to his hiding place, or another he had found on the westerly headland – vantage points to give him a view of whichever route she took, and each arrival and departure. He didn't want to miss anything.

Sometimes, he saw her with the old lady. 'Mad,' they called her in the village. 'A devil, a demon!' To stop them going where they had always gone, to give rats the run of the place, to prefer animals to humans. Yet there they were, arms around each other, walking along the shore from the castle, laughing together; or laughing as they linked hands to shoo a herd of deer away from the incoming tide. But the old lady was never there to watch her swim. Only he did that.

One day, she wasn't there. He waited and waited, but there was no sign of her, at the jetty, or at the beach. He scanned the shore from end to end, but there was nothing. He stayed all morning, not caring about the weight of his father's hand, or his mother's down-turned eyes and mouth. None of that mattered any more.

It was the same the next day, and the next. And the talk in the village grew hushed around him. Had she left without him knowing?

No.

Perhaps it was no more than the storm that was keeping her ashore. The wind had been up, the sea high; too fierce, maybe, even for her. There was one place he couldn't see, hidden by the promontory stretching out from the far side towards the open water, a place the boats stayed away from, on account of the hidden currents and eddies. Perhaps she was staying in the shelter of the bay until the worst of the weather passed.

He would take the boat over, just to make sure.

The gust caught him as he rounded the headland, just after he stood up in the trembling craft, to scan the island. And he was sure he could see her! Not swimming, but on the shore, looking at him looking at her, their eyes meeting, as he had always thought they were.

The boat tipped with him, pulling him under.

It didn't matter. She would come for him, he knew. That was his thought, as the rope wound around his leg, as the weight on his lungs grew heavier. It was nothing to her, to reach him. A few strong strokes, a dip under, and she would wrap her arms around him, and he would feel her naked body close to his, at last. And she would pull him free, and swim with him to the shore. They would lie there together, and he would breathe.

On the rise of the island, the swimmer looked across at the upturned boat. She had been watching it for a while now. The boy, again. She smiled, and turned away.

John Saul

The garden designer

The garden designer came and saw, without conquering. He has put up his car window for the last time. What he did, the garden work aside, was not so much conquering as holding her sway, and now she will have back her sway, to do with as she wants. Moreover her friend Jaz, calling from her palatial spread down the road, has this minute phoned to confirm that he's left the area, gone, taking his raucous laugh, his contrariness and crooked teeth, which is more than she wants to remember of him. A complete explanation for his departure will not be forthcoming, as by now he will be far away in the fens with the eels and canals, the great drains that lead through the mud to the sea—as far as the eye can see he said, redundantly, as if the eye might not see what it saw, and now he was redundant himself, lost to her for good, doubtless back home at the drawing board—so she imagines, as she presses the red button on the phone and stares at it, the crude little symbol, dully registering she hasn't fully noticed it before, he will be visiting locations drumming up business, his silver-grey Passat with the trailer shooting between the sugar beet and cauliflower fields, while she remains in the conservatory in her house on the hill, wondering at the tannin that has spread on the surface of her tea, should she get a spoon to make it go away, what difference would that make, a man, a spoon, it is a desire without purpose, any difference in taste would be marginal at the most; and yet, pitted against the wisdom of her mind is this desire to get a spoon and stir it, a desire that is at odds with the urge to stay put, get up, don't get up, get up, it's a tiring bit of wrestling between the animal and the rational, putting her in mind of Jaz the animal and Jaz's husband Horace, the oh-so-rational Horace. The thought of them is exhausting, having to decide is exhausting. To shelve deciding she stays in her wicker chair hoping to see blackbirds or be approached by a robin, not that she's concentrating on catching sight of either, she's just being there, gazing vacantly at the garden, which the garden designer had not designed so much as shaped up, tidied, laying new paving slabs for old, shoring up the wall. Armed with a spade and fork and strimmer he had professionally smartened things, the monkey puzzle tree she never liked had been smartened, the overhanging branches that used to brush the roof have been cut back, leaving a clean-shaped canopy of leaves, leaves that look a darker green each time she sees them, a dark colour she suspects steeped in venom, while a swing with new rope is hung from the other tree, dangling improbably, awaiting the unlikely appearance of a child; well there is at least the one new feature, the birch, which she had been instructed to take a bucket of water to and sponge down, three trees in a ridiculous space but best not to think of all those roots burrowing everywhere because taken as a whole it worked, good had been done and the pain was almost bearable, maybe the upsides would last longer than the downsides, for one thing he had left this tree, and the wall had been buttressed to stop the whole shebang of earth from shifting down the hill, no doubt aided by worms, to the glee of worms, creatures she quickly associates with the brown stain floating on her tea, as if they would like to see that, anything brown, as if they would be amazed anyone should go over to the kitchen for a spoon to disrupt that lovely surface, they certainly wouldn't bother, their one dedication being to tunnel, and it may have been the word, worm, that made her feel this way, but out of nowhere she was furious at him, and at Jaz and Horace, whose house she could see from here, at least the roof and strip of wall below it. Jaz and Horace had put the designer off from returning, curse them, damn him, the worm, let him come back as a worm, let him be cut in two and see how he gets on then. But what a rigmarole it was, mad, the whole strung-out tale, what mad thoughts she had, gazing now at the wall, admittedly the repairs he had made were nicely grouted, the house was slipping nowhere, and but for the newly buttressed wall it could have, the wall leaning into the hill where windmills once turned, gaily she imagines, in some quiet old world, she imagines, allowing bits and pieces she had read to join up in some romantic view of the past, oh well, there is the tree, and yes the wall does its job, as a lasting bulwark, preventing the garden from starting a local avalanche, the earth bursting to cross the road, all of which she is grateful for, but only up to a point grateful, after all she paid him to do it, everything strictly according to the contract, she had even written *and board* into the agreement, not guessing board would turn into bed, and as for the upshot, through the conservatory window the garden is in front of her, the one tidy thing in the middle of the great mess, but it is still too small a garden to do much in, despite being shaped up, speaking of which she should shape up, so to make a start she puts both hands on her ribs, breathes in deeply, breathes out, slowly in, out, looks down at the table, pulls the teabag from her cup with her fingers, hurries to the outside door so it won't drip, already there's some on her trainers, she tosses the teabag as if alive towards the rose bush before hastening back to the chair and her tea, now without its patch of tannin, her homogenous tea on the table with its amateurish mosaic, admittedly garish, I should change that table he had said to her the very first day of his work, what a cheek, no wonder he was into design, wanting to reshape everything in sight, the question now was what real impact had he had, the sex aside, she would rather not recollect the sex, what was it, the garden aside, what had he brought to her that would leave a stamp, possibly for ever, well there was a moment that stood out, a beacon, shedding light onto a realisation in the darkness, an important realisation she feels she should stand to announce, and stand she does, glimpsing the head of the postman above the wall, the tall postman in a cap with the stubbly skin, stubbly grin, so what was it, well, the trick to it all lay with the plans themselves, finely pencilled like the work of an architect, it was the plans for her patch that persuaded her friends the Parmentiers, *former* friends the Parmentiers, Horace and Jaz, and particularly Jaz, since who knows what Horace thought, Horace was so seldom vocal, according to Jaz he was too busy fussing over whether the pictures on their walls were straight, the collars of his shirts had their buttons done, or if all the coat hangers hung the same way, You can have him Jaz said, if you want a man with the heart of a clock, take him, for Horace rarely said a word, as if he needed a lifetime to cope with having been called that name. But to return to the light shed by the beacon, it was the plans for her wall on the outsized papers, the clever cross-section, the faint but clear pencilling, the sheets pinned down by books at the corners, that her friend Jaz was enthusing over, ex friend was enthusing over, her friend no more now that she has scared the garden designer away, Oh wouldn't it be lovely to have our garden planned, Horace, these drawings are so delightful, look that's a birch, *Horace*, we could have the pond I always wanted, we could have a hut for you, oh how Jaz would like to siphon him off to a shed, *to a shed* she says out loud to the glass panes of the conservatory, before sitting back down, examining the cup handle for cracks, staring at the maligned mosaic which until the designer came she never used to care much about, one way or the other, Jaz had been so enthusiastic, no wait, now that their friendship had swilled down the drain she didn't like to think *enthusiastic*, she had been *gushing*, disgustingly, since in fact what she was after was not a garden revamp or even a plan, an idea that could be framed and hung to prompt the occasional con-versation, what she was reaching for was the garden designer himself, in accordance with her lust, the rampant lust of Jaz Parmentier which now was common knowledge—all right known, since her visit that afternoon, to them both—because when Jaz caught wind of *her* own, ultimately brief affair with the designer, possibly scotching designs of hers, she said rather quickly how there were many fish in the sea and she herself was a good swimmer, excellent swimmer, and after having a go on the new swing, just there, thrusting herself sexually forward, Jaz spilled more of her many beans, they showered out in sackfuls, how she liked to go from one warm bed to another; the return of these words put her in mind of clean white sheets, the picture of which swept aside thoughts of a second cup of tea, a marshmallow?, *Jaz* wouldn't go for a marsh-mallow, not in the context of sitting looking at a garden, no, not for Jaz cups of tea sat in a conservatory when she could head down the motorway or sweep off to an international airport lounge, hand luggage only, ready to camp out at some attractive location, Cornwall or the Lakes and in the USA motels and tents on Fire Island, wherever that may be, and these were merely examples, so no, not for her would time be spent sponging down a birch tree, not when she could be at another Bon Jovi concert, that being the way she went about things, so Jaz told her in confidence, some sort of confidence, not

strict confidence, told her how she got what she wanted
via Jon Bon Jovi, off she would go to the concerts and
mingle with his audiences, after which and even during
which it was not Jon Bon Jovi himself but the lingering
thought of him that she imposed, superimposed, on
anyone within half a mile of him, she tried the same
with Bruce Springsteen but eventually his age did for
him, Springsteen who had his moments, the same
became of Neil Young before him, she had settled for
JBJ and his disciples, and next in line, as if he hadn't
been catered for already, was the garden designer, a no-
contest with the alternative being Horace, Horace, she
can visualise his brogues and turn-ups, who in the world
wants Horace, she struggled to deal with the enormity
of Jaz hopping here there and everywhere, as she said,
from one warm bed to the next, but out it all came,
voilà, this was how Jaz presented her secret self, at this
very table, stupid table, and then *she* in her turn passed
on these secrets to the designer as they lay in bed, faces
close, no longer discussing washing down the birch tree,
or shades of grouting, how the monkey puzzle got its
name, not laughing or playing either, he commented
this friend of hers was the locust of love, circling the
earth, something about it disturbed him, he said, not
saying what, but he wasn't sure he wanted to take on
their commission down the road after all, he might just
make the plans and leave it at that, now that he'd heard
the scale of the adultery, adulteries; those two, the man
and wife in name only, could be headed for the rocks,
in the middle of which recollection she decides in
favour of the marshmallow so goes quickly to the
kitchen and fetches the packet, but on returning the
sudden warmth of the conservatory makes her sleepy,
she dozes, nods awake, the memories were becoming
too many and too heavy, she struggles to resume where

she left off, as if talking to herself was a conversation on a thread that shouldn't break, gropes to go back where she was, yes, the locust of love: the phrase bothered her, that was what she was thinking, it didn't sound right at all, it was irritating, and suddenly everything was irritating, no birds came by, clouds kept holding back the sun, the last of the tea was cold, best to counter the irritation with action, so she got up again and tossed the last of it towards the rose bush, feeling an unannounced pang about the garden designer, in the midst of which there arrived the memory of him laying out the sets of plans for her modest patch, which was to lead on his next visit to laying out the much grander plans for Jaz and Horace, because he did go ahead with them after all, at least with the planning stage, though that was as far as it went, she remembered the papers being unrolled on the Parmentiers' table, she imagined them on the mosaic table when suddenly a bar of sunlight caught her eye, lighting a length of wall, where a robin hopped and danced for no obvious purpose, and the robin and the brickwork glowed redly together, pleased both to be in the sun and see their colours acknowledged, it was at *this* table the *idea* for plans of their own surfaced, You are such a chatterbox Jaz said to Horace, scathingly of course, as he shrugged at the idea of scheming with their garden, why *wouldn't* you like a beautiful garden, say something, say *yes*, yes darling, but Horace reacted only by scratching his head, and with hindsight this was clearly a run-up to the designer making his final visit, with his plans for them, drawings to outstrip those he made for her, and from there to the crucial turning point, the pivot they all four swung about, the roundabout which suddenly stopped, and here she pictured it turning faster and faster, as they all four swung around with their legs pulled outwards, hanging on by the shoulder sockets, because Jaz had gone ahead to commission him, and in spite of his misgivings, lured perhaps by the substantial sum of money, the garden designer soon took off in a silver-grey flash to return one week later, when he briskly went once around the garden with the strimmer, repeated his remark on the mosaic table top, and twisted then pushed the swing, she remembered how side by side they watched the back and forth but without their arms around each other, then back inside he washed up and ate and they went to bed for what would be the last night before the morning after, the last morning, when they walked down and up the dip in the earth to the Parmentier's, he with a netted bag of cabbages grown on the fens and, rolled up in tubes, the lovely, even finer plans for Jaz and Horace, the size of their garden had some scope and the plans reflected that, with delicate pencilling showing the pond, the cobblestones he called setts, the sight lines, the steps at staggered intervals down the paths because everything in this town of theirs was on a hill, and no sooner had the cabbages been dumped in the kitchen, humped in on his shoulder like kittens before being downed, that they four marvelled at these new plans, the clever combination of the wild flowing and the straight-lined, her hand touched his as they set out the books to hold down the corners, yet he gave no sign back to her, instead he continued to effuse over the details, taking his time moving from the pond to the hut to the raised beds he had in mind, he would organise railway sleepers for the purpose, and so on, until he brought up the matter of the sight lines and they moved to check these for themselves in the actual physical world, which was when they looked out, the designer in sudden app-rehension, on the waste land of the Parmentier's garden plot, as it was then and still is now, more plot than garden, at the white squares of plastic Horace had laid on the ground, covering every millimetre of earth and grass, as if he were Christo and Jaz Jeanne-Claude and here was their wrapped garden, the domestical sequel to their wrapped Reichstag. If Horace were to speak, he might have compared the sight to the mats used by nomadic tribesmen, saying they were only temporary; if he had been more Christo than he was Horace, he might have broken his silence to declare the transience of life itself, how nothing is forever, look to every corner of our plot and of course the wrapping will disappear, like our childhood, our lives, whereas what he actually said was, dumbfounding them all: *To keep out the sycamore seeds*, words which put her in mind of the joke about tearing up pieces of paper to keep away elephants, except there was no joke, just crumbly words which he expelled as if on rationed air, so many cubic centimetres a day and that's your lot, parched-sounding words filled with dust between the syllables, dust brought up from his lungs, To keep them out, he reiterated, placing a sudden aggression on the *out*, and she could tell the garden designer was wondering what he'd walked into, as the remark and the desultory sight spread doubt everywhere, even onto the plans on the kitchen table, which were no longer the same precious scrolls, no longer shining with the lustre of moments before but starting to roll up of their own accord, as doubt travelled up and down their plot of ground in waves, so she felt it, this inexplicable development, it spread worst of all onto herself, since Horace and Jaz were supposedly her friends and maybe had a hinge loose, since they were definitely mad, and moreover in two mad worlds, Horace bent on whipping phantoms into line, Jaz with her tour of the world's beds, her Bon

Jovi nights away, pretending she was with her friend two streets from this surreal plot of ground, telling her husband to his face she was sleeping over at her friend's with the little garden, in the room above the conservatory, which is how Jaz's exploits were first known to her, surely Horace didn't really buy these alibis but maybe he did, he could easily have checked but he was no telephoner, as that involved speech, meanwhile his wife was flying the Atlantic and even Pacific if the latest string of tour dates pointed her in the direction, she doubted Jaz had given him wind of any of it, it was unimaginable it cvcr came close to being the subject of conversation at the marital breakfast table, if there was a subject at all, across a toast rack with identically sized triangular slices of bread and a boiled egg, its boiling time controlled minutely by mad professor Parmentier, no, straight after the inc-ident with the sycamore seeds, I remember, she said to herself as she sat down again in the conservatory, I whisked the designer away, back here, where just for lunch I cooked up beans with chillies and dollops of crême fraiche, like snow on the volcano, a little parsley on top to make it pretty, like grass at the crater top, from his silver-grey estate car he even produced and in a haste which she had no explanation for grated some Yarg, a cheese which had been wrapped in nettle leaves but was no longer dangerous, he said, much as he would have liked it to still be dangerous, he added, then said Something had to explode he said, I wish I knew what he was referring to but even after the torrent of explanations he came out with later I don't, I don't know, and for the moment he seemed almost as dumb as Horace, for the moment he simply said what he said, while the morning still reeked of a debacle, and for the last time we took each other in the living room, me thinking this would diminish the significance of having two mad people for friends and put him and her back on course, she remembered, ah, if only it were so, but the fact was it didn't feel quite right, the numbingness spread by the plastic wrapping in the Parmentier garden had got into everything and rubbed off on him and on her, this was a fact, a hard thing, and now there were a number of facts, another being the designer was not beyond being a bit of controller himself, was indeed full of himself—such a contrast to, and such a mismatch for Horace, Horace who was so empty of himself. It had occurred to her too, that since Jaz was shagging adherers of Bon Jovi and could likely be thousands of miles over the horizon when the payment was due, while Horace could be committed to an institution, etcetera, the whole arrangement could turn out to be as shaky as a moth in a flame, but even if these fears weren't convincing it was clear the designer no longer had his heart in returning her way, which meant the only missing fact remaining was did Horace know about Jaz and Bon Jovi and in the past Bruce Springsteen and before him Neil Young, who but Horace could say and he never said anything; she looked across to the swing with the new rope and wondered if a person could hang themselves from it, they could, she could write to the garden designer asking his opinion, ask him to draw some noose knots, she should have asked at the time, before he went off on the road north, looking troubled, waiting until the last minute to come out with the torrent she'd been referring to, out it came as he wound down his window for the last time, Even before I went ahead with the plans I thought this garden project could get hairy, what with the wild woman expecting herons to dive into her pond and Horace ready to get on the phone at the first buzz of a fly, I did what I could but where is the design to satisfy those contradictory forces, he said with his hand on the ignition key, the man wanted not one weed, not a leaf, while she was all for snakes and alligators, no the plastic wasn't some little thing, it was a message loud and clear, it would stop anyone in their tracks, didn't she agree? he said finally, which was when she realised he was abandoning the project, they would not be taking each other on the rug again, or at the armchair either, which had actually been rather awkward but there you go, what has the rug got to do with it, what has love got to do with it, it was over in no time and no use now recalling how the bits of clothing had got strewn around, including his shirt which had narrowly missed being set fire to by the Aga, which wasn't in fact an Aga but that's what he called it, as if he could reshape the universe, like some modern-day Midas. I have to say, said the designer taking a final glance towards the roof and the monkey puzzle tree, that Horace filled me with dismay, I may live in the fens but what people get up to down here, this life in the shires, I'm best out of it don't you think? he concluded, and as he pushed the button to pull up the window she bit her lip rather than point out he lived in a shire himself, then when he wound the window down again to reach out and adjust his wing mirror, oh so you will be looking back now and then will you she was tempted to say but bit back the words, and when again the window wound up she only narrowly avoided screaming he could go now, just go, back to the turnips and potatoes—and the tulips, he would have only added. Whatever got said it was as good as over, wasted, was it wasted, if she wanted to dig up a counter-weight there were the tendernesses too, lying thinking of the cigarettes they said they would have had post-coitally in a bygone era, in the years between the windmills and the present, though even then he said he'd like a change made to the wallpaper, Strip it down and paint it white he said, And that pastel of a cornfield on the wall should be in a black frame not gold, even then she had kidded herself to think there was mileage in it yet, in him, still she thought they might lie there exploring each other like monkeys, without a thought for Jaz and Horace and what garden designs they might want or not want, although the Parmentier differences had somehow destroyed the project, she should have guessed the second wave of the business would be too tricky, would never get anywhere and it didn't, and when that was obvious to them all, Jaz included, Jaz especially, oh boy, someone was going to get it, that someone had to be Horace, who was foolish enough to point out an error Jaz had made in how to hang up the washing, for which he had a regimen, not with clothes pegs indoors was his rule, and if the clothes pegs were not used they would have longer lives, that is, the pegs would have, saving them the futility of financing all the industries that had nothing better to do than make clothes pegs all day, so could she please stop, which was when Jaz—so she told her—finally gave explosive vent to her frustrations, her rage, and confess to the Bon Jovi concerts, how she channelled the desperate crushes she had on the famous, how she had been covering her tracks, even who in the audiences touched who, and how, even as they stood or danced, out it came, the cities were named, the motels were described, the exhilarations and sadnesses, the situations the following mornings, upon which, Jaz told her, Horace turned his back and went upstairs to bed, without a word.

Notes on Contributors

JL Bogenschneider is a writer of short fiction, with work published in a number of print and online journals, including The Aleph, Cosmonauts Avenue, Strix, Isthmus, 404 Ink, PANK and Ambit.

Ursula Brunetti is a Faber Academy graduate from the Isle of Wight. Her fiction has been shortlisted for the Harper's Bazaar Short Story Competition 2019 and longlisted for the Royal Society of Literature's V.S. Pritchett Short Story Competition 2019. She has been published by Popshot, The Londonist, Fairlight Books, Liar's League and Cinnamon Press. She is currently working on a novel and short story collection.

Gina Challen: Born in London, Gina moved to West Sussex in 1979. Although originally a city girl, the Downlands stole her heart, and are the inspiration for her writing. She holds a Masters Degree in Creative Writing from the University of Chichester. Her work can be found in *The Bristol Short Story Prize Volume 8,* the *Willesden Herald New Short Stories 8 & 9*, The Cinnamon Press Short Story Award anthologies 2012 & 2013 and *Rattle Tales 2.* Two stories were shortlisted for the prestigious Bridport Prize and in 2018 a further story was longlisted for the RSL, V S Pritchett Price. Other stories are online with Seren Books, Ink Tears and Storgy magazines, and her critical essays at Thresholds Short Story Forum. Her collection of short stories, *Chalk Tracks,* was published in July 2019. She can be found at www.ginachallen.co.uk. @ginabchallen

Carol Dines lives in Minneapolis and has recently finished a collection of stories, *Distance of Closeness*. Several stories from the new collection have been published. She has also published two novels for young adults, *Best Friends Tell the Best Lies (Delacorte), The Queen's Soprano (Harcourt)* and a collection of short stories for Young Adults, *Talk to Me (Delacorte.)* In addition, she has published numerous poems and stories in magazines and anthologies.

Derek Dirckx is a writer living in St. Paul, Minnesota, in the United States. He's studied writing most recently at the Loft Literary Center. This is his first publication.

Sarah Evans has had many short stories published in anthologies, literary journals and online. Her stories have been shortlisted by the Commonwealth Short Story Prize and awarded prizes by, amongst others: Words and Women, Stratford Literary Festival and the Bridport Prize. Her work is also included in several Unthology volumes, Best New Writing and Shooter Magazine.

Jeff Ewing is the author of the short story collection *The Middle Ground*, published by Into the Void Press. His fiction, poetry, and essays have appeared in Crazyhorse, Southwest Review, ZYZZYVA, Willow Springs, Subtropics, and Saint Ann's Review. He lives in Sacramento, California with his wife and daughter.

David Frankel is a writer and artist. His short stories have been published in anthologies and magazines including Unthology 8, Lightship and The London Magazine. He has been shortlisted for a number of competitions including The Bath Short Story Award,

The Willesden Herald, The Hilary Mantel Short Story Competition, and The Fish Memoir Competition. His MA in creative writing, from Chichester University, was awarded the Kate Betts Memorial Prize. David was born in Salford and now lives in Kent.

Ray French writes fiction, memoir and essays. He was born in Wales to Irish parents and a central preoccupation is the experience of being torn between two cultures. He is the co-editor of *I Wouldn't Start From Here: The Second Generation Irish in Britain* and *End Notes: Ten Stories About Loss, Mourning and Commemoration.* He is the author of *The Red Jag & other stories* and the novels *All This Is Mine* and *Going Under.* He is one of four male authors featured in *Four Fathers,* a collection of memoirs about having and being a father. His short story 'Migration' was included in *Best European Fiction 2013.*

N. Jane Kalu is a Nigerian woman, a short story writer, scriptwriter, and playwright. Her work has appeared in Munyori Journal, Kalahari Review, Jalada, and others. In 2015, she was shortlisted for the Writivism short story prize. She's currently an MFA student and Core Writing Instructor at the University of New Mexico. She's known on social media as @njanekalu.

Marylee MacDonald is a former carpenter and author of *Bonds of Love and Blood,* *Montpelier Tomorrow,* and *The Rug Bazaar.* Her short stories have won the Barry Hannah Prize, the Jeanne M. Leiby Memorial Chapbook Award, the Matt Clark Prize, the Ron Rash Award, the American Literary Review Fiction Prize, and come in 2nd and 3rd in the Faulkner-Wisdom Short Story Competition. Her fiction has appeared in American Literary Review, New Delta Review, North

Atlantic Review, Ruminate, The Bellevue Literary Review, StoryQuarterly, The Briar Cliff Review, The Chattahoochee Review, The Sandy River Review, The Superstition Review, Yalobusha Review, and more. "Caboose" is one of the stories in her forth-coming short story collection, *Body Language*.

Jaki McCarrick is an award-winning writer of plays, poetry and fiction. Her play LEOPOLDVILLE won the 2010 Papatango Prize for New Writing, and her most recent play, THE NATURALISTS, premiered in New York to enthusiastic reviews in the New York Times, The New Yorker and elsewhere. Her play BELFAST GIRLS was developed at the National Theatre Studio, London, and was shortlisted for the 2012 Susan Smith Blackburn Prize and the 2014 BBC Tony Doyle Award. It premiered in the US in Chicago to much critical acclaim. Her short story "The Visit" won the 2010 Wasafiri Short Fiction Prize and appears in the 2012 Anthology of Best British Short Stories (Salt). Jaki's short story collection *The Scattering (Seren Books)* was shortlisted for the 2014 Edge Hill Prize.

Gerard McKeown's work has been featured in The Moth, 3:AM, and Litro, among others. In 2017 he was shortlisted for The Bridport Prize, and in 2018 he was longlisted for The Irish Book Awards' Short Story of the Year. His story Detachment was recently featured in the anthology *Still Worlds Turning (No Alibis Press)*.

Jay Merill lives in London UK and is Writer in Residence at Women in Publishing. Jay was runner up in the 2018 International Alpine Fellowship Writing Prize, a Pushcart Prize nominee and the winner of the Salt short story Prize. She is the author of two collections,

God of the Pigeons and *Astral Bodies,* and has work published or forthcoming in literary magazines, including 3:AM, Crannog, Prairie Schooner, SmokeLong Quarterly and a list of over twenty more.

Diana Powell's stories have won, or been featured, in a number of competitions, including the 2019 ChipLit Festival Prize (winner), and the 2014 Penfro award (winner). They have also appeared in a variety of journals and anthologies, including The Lonely Crowd, Crannog and The Blue Nib. Her novella, *Esther Bligh* was published last year by Holland House Books, and her short story collection *Trouble Crossing the Bridge* will be published in December by the Blue Nib Press.

John Saul made the contribution from England to the Best European Fiction 2018 anthology published by Dalkey Archive (in previous years: AS Byatt, Hilary Mantel). In the UK his short fiction has been brought together in four collections. He was shortlisted for the international 2015 Seán Ó Faoláin prize, was runner-up in the 2018 Forge short fiction competition and had work included in Best British Short Stories 2016. He is a member of the European Literature Network. www.johnsaul.co.uk.

Lightning Source UK Ltd.
Milton Keynes UK
UKHW010622040320
359745UK00001B/1

9 780999 527764